Reviews for King Pant

I hadn't realised that fall down the cellar steps when Noel was a toddler would have such a long-term effect on the poor boy.
Mrs Josie Brennan (Noel's Mum)

I, for one, don't believe a word of it. I think he made the whole thing up.
Michael Brennan (Noel's brother)

Oh dad! Why are you sooo embarrassing!
(Noel's ungrateful kids)

They say that if you don't use it, you lose it. Well, this just shows that Noel never had it in the first place.
Marjerine Grimmer (Noel's English teacher, year 9)

Much funnier than that Shakespeare bloke.
Steven Fry (aged 4)

Foresooth that inddeedely be a bit rude.
William Shakespeare (deceased)

Noel has magically woven a string of incomprehensible sentences into a storyline thinner that the earth's outer atmosphere.
Ermatrude Q Welliron (Astronomer Royal, chip shop owner and part time pantomime horse's rear end)

I bought it on Kindle, so I can't even use it to light the fire.
Clarentine Dotsprocket (Author of *Therapy for Those Beyond Help*)

Would be much better if Noel had left the pages blank, at least that way my three-year old niece could have used it as a scribble pad.
Randox Seablanket (made up person)

The perfect stocking filler for someone you don't like.
Bargain Grabber TV Christmas Special

It's got everything, words, pictures, characters and a story. They just need rearranging into something that makes sense!
Filo Ladlefork (Author of *How to be a clever book critic*)

Someone once said that inside every person there is a great book just waiting to be written.
I have made it my mission to prove that person wrong.

Noel J Brennan

Chapter 1

Once upon a Smelly Market

And it was a very smelly market. It had that kind of eye-watering smell that makes you not only block your nose, but your ears as well just in case the offending odour somehow manages to seep in that way instead. It was smelly and busy, and funny-looking men with funny-looking noses shouted and argued with each other in really loud voices.

'Two rangles for a Eudar?' spat a man with a turnip-shaped nose.

'Gerraway. They was only five shepples yesterday!'

'Should've got one yesterday then,' sniffed a carrot-nosed Eudar seller, swinging a squawking specimen by its scraggy scrotum.

'Well, are you 'aving one or not?'

'Ees is eight shepples,' called a man with a nose like a tulip, 'and ees is fatter!'

'Who's is?'

'Him over there, him 'as got a nose like a dog!'

'Ees are only fatter on the outside, mine's fatter on the inside,' Carrotnose protested.

He did have a point. His Eudars did look fatter on the inside.

'If you want my advice, you should never trust a man with a nose like an animal,' added a man with a nose like a pig.

The senseless wrangling raged on and on like every other day in the smelly market square, drowning out the ranting, stamping and shouting that was coming from inside the Castle.

But then again nobody ever took much notice of what went on inside the Castle.

Chapter 2

Inside the Castle (as if anyone cared)

'**PANTS!**'

King Edgar was in a mood. He had a broad spectrum of moods depending on what kind of mood he was in. Todays was deepest black and had stuck to the King all day like a stick of old black sticky liquorice that had been nailed on with magnetic superglue. He'd sulked, shouted and stamped all morning, taken a break to enjoy a light lunch of roasted Eudar with crabby-yam fries and rhubarberry ice-cream, then stamped, shouted and sulked some more. He'd even uttered the 'really bad' swear word (yes, that one) but still it didn't make any difference.

King Edgar of Evermore (as in 'happily ever after', the elusive realm of fairy tales) had recently acquired an unfortunate tendency to use, reuse and overuse the word '**pants**' as an expletive. He thought it was funny.

This, along with a penchant for wearing vivid, tasteless and ill-fitting trousers is what had led to the nickname 'King Pants' in the first place. Its famed usage had now spread far beyond the confines of the Castle walls. Even the local school children could be heard merrily singing this sweet playground ditty:

Old King Pants wears silly old pants,
And 'silly old pants' says he.
He ain't got a chance
Of going to the dance.
And his pants are just funnee- ee.

There are approximately eighty-seven more verses of *Old King Pants* all of which are just as bad as the first, but we haven't got time for that now.

King Pants remained blissfully unaware of this however as he rarely ventured outside the Castle. This evening in an attempt to soothe his tattered nerves, he flicked listlessly through a sagging shelf of CDs (ask your parents, they'll know). He chanced upon a copy of *Please Don't Blame the Music* by The Voice of Reason (a favourite of his father Ole King Cole who died young due to a chronic bout of hedonism). I haven't listened to The Voice of Reason for years, thought the King, and I'm not going to start now. Recklessly he tossed the CD case over his shoulder. It rebounded off a statue of a naked man wrestling a potato, double flipped onto a servant (who looked like a potato) and bounced off a portrait of 'Dad', the merry old soul, before smashing against a really big hard wall.

KErrrrrrrACK!

Two seconds later another handful of rejects whizzed through the air.

'PANTS!' *SMermmmmACK!*
'BORING!' *PErrrrrrrrrrrrANG!*

'#**#!' (unprintable – insert your favourite naughty word).

'RUBBISH!'

'What is?' chipped in Queen Bob, 'Your hair?'

'No no NO! This.....these!'

He glared down at his hands like someone had just put dog dirt in them.

'Hey, relax – don't take your bad mood out on them old CDs!' said the Queen going back to what she had been doing - painting her toenails Putrid Plum while humming the theme tune to Joust of the Day,

'Di-di-di dee di-di-di di-dee, di-dee di-di-di dee' (you know how it goes).

'You're right, they are old' said the King as though the terrible truth fairy had sprayed **'*now there's a thing!*'** on the inside of his eyelids. With a sigh King Pants slid to the floor and scowled at the little plastic tiles with a mixture of distain and despair.

'Tom Tom was good, could have been one of the greats...' he mused. 'But after that incident with the pig his career never stood a chance. And as for Humperty flippin' Dumperdink, he was certainly not all he was...'

'Cracked up to be!' quipped Queen Bob, stealing his punch line (even though she knew Edgar's jokes were never quite as funny as that bloke's on the telly).

'To think, I used to prize myself on having the finest music collection in the Kingdom,' King Pants lamented. 'Now Sleeping Beauty's *Wake Up Sleepy Dreamer* just makes me *YAWN*. Rapunzel's Hair is a *LET DOWN*...'

'Wee Willy-Winky's got a new single out. Have you heard it?' the Queen interjected.

The very mention of Wee Willy was enough to tip King Pants over the edge. His eyes swelled like a couple of ripe pimples, a vein in this neck jigged like a drowning leprechaun, his teeth grated, a bead of saliva swung from his bottom lip and his ears fluttered with rage. Shakes turned to twitches, twitches turned to spasms then the room exploded in a hail of sweat and spit, flying CDs and unrepeatable language.

WErrrrrAZZZ!
KErrrrrrrrrrrrrrrrrrrrrrrrrrrrrrBAMAZZZ!

BOOrrrrrrrrOOMKABrrrrrACKAZZ!

A barrage of furious plastic ricocheted between the walls. Guards ducked for cover under tables and behind curtains. A naked man grabbed the potato-faced servant, wrestling him to the floor. Flying discs shot through windows, doors, keyholes and mouseholes. The frenzied episode lasted for five minutes and thirty-seven seconds precisely after which the King slumped into a crumpled heap sobbing breathlessly.

'And another thing....' he said wiping his runny nose, 'Why did you have to buy that ostrich?'

'Because he can talk.' replied the Queen.

'This is Evermore,' he sighed. 'Everything can talk!'

'Yes, but he can talk sense.'

Queen Bob opened a bottle of beer with her teeth, burped heartily and settled down to her *Let's all Laugh at a Loaded*

Celebrity magazine. 'And let's face it, there's not much sense to be found in these parts of late.'

'Indeed' agreed Aspinol as he pecked at the broken bits of plastic wedged in his feathers. 'Never was a truer word spoken.'

He was an ostrich of some breeding.

Chapter 3

Back at the Smelly Market

Bedlam and chaos are not the only words to describe the scene in the market square. There's also havoc, mayhem and pandemonium if you really want to show off. The crowds had looked to the heavens in utter disbelief as a cloudburst of plastic shards and shiny discs came raining from the sky like a biblical plague. Hundreds, thousands of them.

There was a mad scramble as people filled their pockets, buckets, wheelbarrows and wardrobes with the bountiful offering. Benjamin Bigmouth managed to filch the complete *This Old Man* back catalogue, stashing it away under his tongue (and that's no mean feat, even for Benjamin). The 'Great, Magnificent and a Little Bit Frightening CD Storm' (as it came to be known) lasted for two whole days and nights according to legend. Three months later a rare, signed copy of *I kissed a girl* by Georgie Porgie was found in a tree by a man with an odd-looking nose.

For a while the people in the smelly market forgot all about the smell, the pushing, shoving, arguing and shouting as they jostled about, pushing, shoving, arguing and shouting.

A fight broke out when a man with a dog nose punched a man on his carrot nose.

'Ow me nose, Gerroff!'

'That really hurt.'

'Shurrup!'

'Oy!'

'GRAB THART EUDARRRR!!!!'

Amidst the fracas a renegade group of Eudars seized the opportunity to break free and flee the marketplace, eventually finding sanctuary on the cold, wet, northern-most moorlands of Yorkersham and adopting the motto 'Eudars wins'

Chapter 4

The Great Hall (just down the corridor)

Aspinol in his wisdom and because he was hungry had sounded the great dinner gong earlier than usual by spitting a well sucked bobo nut at it. *Ping!* It usually went *Bong!* But bobo nuts are very small.

'Good shot old bird.' He said, patting himself on the back of his immaculate plumage with his tiny useless wing. Eudar was off the menu, due to an unforeseen shortage of the little hairy blighters, so a great tureen of bum-warm Thickerty Stew was served up instead.

'Pah!' pah-ed the King hoping someone would hear him. 'Not thicking Thickerty Stew again!' In truth his black mood had lifted slightly only to be replaced by one of a more menacing muddy-grey hue. Like that itchy sweater your mother made you wear to your least favourite Aunty's house on a hot day. Itchy and hot and the neck and wrist holes are too tight and it itches and it's grey.

'PAH!'

'Whatever has got into you today, Eddie?' snapped Queen Bob. 'Me and Aspinol...'

'Aspinol and I,' corrected the ostrich.

'Aspinol and I,' continued the Queen 'we was..'

'We were'

'*Arrrghhh!*'

Just as she was about to speak again a man holding a bloody nose appeared at the window.

'Good grief, who's that subject with the nasal haemorrhage?' shrieked Aspinol.

'I don't know,' the Queen glowered, 'Better get him a tissue.'

'Probably some common market trader,' remarked the King. 'They're always fighting and appearing in windows and trying to sell you things when you're not looking. Tell him we don't want any bloody carrots today.'

King Pants had no time or sympathy for commoners with bleeding noses, carrot-shaped or otherwise. He had something else on his mind.

'It's all a load of old pants,' he spat, throwing down his fork and spoon.

'*PANTS, PANTS, PANTS!*'

'Will you stop saying that!' sighed the Queen, throwing a Mint Royale cholocude in the air and catching it in her mouth. 'Don't you care what they all say about you? *Old King Pants wears silly old pants... and silly old pants says he...*' she sang in a baby voice.

'Stop it!' the King looked mortally offended. 'I'm talking about the music. The vibes, the sounds, the beats, man. It's all so.... YESTERYEAR!'

The Queen picked up her pipe, overstuffed it with smelly tobacco and glared at the King.

'Are you still going on about those silly CDs? You can always go into town and buy some more tomorrow, and while you're at it get something done with your hair.'

'Do you think he's having a mid-reign crisis?' whispered Aspinol to the Queen as he leaned in with a lighter. 'Shall I call the doctor?'

The King had now climbed onto the table and was waving his wibbly-wobbly arms wildly. His eyes were closed as though he was conducting an invisible orchestra of badly tuned bogpipes.

'Not new CDs, I want some *NEW MUSIC!*' he bawled.

'What you need,' suggested Aspinol holding out his wing to help the King down, 'Is an event that presents an opportunity for the musically gifted to compete against each another in order to demonstrate their ability.'

'I know!' said the Queen, wiping her glucky mouth with the back of her velvet sleeve. 'How about a talent competition? You can judge the singing Eddie, and I can judge the... er hem... talent! *WHEY-HEY!*' Queen Bob made an unladylike gesture involving a bent arm and a fist.

'BRILLIANT!' the Kings eyes bugged out like pop gun bubble gum bubbles about to pop. 'Bob, you're a genius.' He would have leapt across the table and kissed her if she hadn't got Thickerty Stew on her chin, chocolude goo on her teeth and pipe smoke coming out of her nostrils.

'A talent competition is just what we need.' He began to pace the room with renewed vigour, stroking his fluffy stubble purposefully as though milking it for inspiration. 'Aspinol, send a royal decree throughout the land. I want a band of noble knights to embark on a great quest across the kingdom.'

'Yers... your Majesty. Or perhaps I could just place an advert in **The Evermore Gazette?**'

'Splendid. I could get my mate Pete in as a judge too. He's a bigwig in the music industry.'

'PETE?' Queen Bob glanced up suddenly. 'You mean Pete with the green tights? Botox buttocks? Tell me you're joking! You know he's slicker than a greased slime eel.'

(Slime eels inhabit the muddy banks of the river Oooze that wends its way merrily through the discarded shopping carts of Evermore. For many years very clever swotty-boffin types with clipboards have tried to study these amazing creatures, but because they are so slimy nobody has ever been able to catch one.)

'Who? May I enquire?' asked Aspinol.

'Yes. Pete Piper. He's perfect for a bit of razzle and quite a lot of dazzle. Bob, if I remember rightly, you were quite taken with him once upon a time.'

'He's a prat, him and that daft flute. Have you forgotten it's his fault we've been landed with all those Filthy Lurkers.' The Queen stood up and began scratching her armpits in irritation. 'I preferred the rats.'

'RATS! Could somebody please explain?' Aspinol was starting to flap, suddenly remembering he had a perfectly rational fear of rodents.

But the King had raced out of the room muttering something under his breath about an old phone book, and Queen Bob was already kicking a servant up the corridor.

'Who, what, rats, where?' said a bewildered Aspinol spinning around and realising he was all alone.

Chapter 5

Down in the Cellar

A couple of cheeky mouslets were lying in a bed of long-forgotten rubbish at the end of an endlessly gloomy corridor deep in the bowels of the Castle's underbelly.

'Giggle, giggle,' giggled the first mouslet.

His friend had just let out a squeaky little fart and the whole corridor stank (though not unpleasantly if you are a mouslet) of half-digested leftover Thickerty Stew.

'Giggle, giggle,' giggled the offender, to her shame she was the larger of the two and should have known better. 'Go on it's your turn now!'

Standing in the shadows the Castle's mousleteer, known as 'Cat' was watching, waiting and holding his nose. Skulking in the rank murkiness at the nether end of the corridor lurked a Filthy Lurker. A big one. A big hungry one. And there is no better meal for a Filthy Lurker than Thickerty Stew wrapped in mouslet, wrapped in mousleteer. (That is apart from Eudar, which had become something of a delicacy as you don't see many around here anymore).

Suddenly, quicker than a turbo-charged turbot (it's a fish, look it up) a hairy blood-soaked hand shot out from yet another shadow and grabbed the Filthy Lurker by its filthy neck.

Before he had time to even think 'Blimey, there I was athinkin' I was gonna get me'sen a right gud meal in me belly when some great 'airy blood-soaked hand comes out n' grabs us, and is probly gonna shove us in an ol' sack wi' a load of other Filthy Lurkers!' he was shoved in a sack with a load of other Filthy Lurkers.'

'Evening Boys!'

'Evening Fred! How's the kids?'

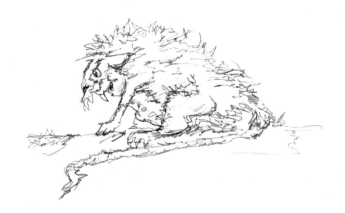

Chapter 6

In a Land Far, Far Away

Aphone trilled in its cradle. *I'm a phone, I'm a phone hear me ring*, sang the happy little handset. Ever so casually a well-manicured hand reached out and lifted the receiver to a well-manicured ear.

'Piper Music, Pete speaking, International Agent to International Stars.'

Pete Piper was sitting in his huge executive chair in front of his enormous executive desk surrounded by gold discs, awards and trophies of all shapes and sizes; Best Bands, Best Music, Most No1's, BEST RAT CATCHER although he preferred to keep that one hidden behind SHINIEST TEETH. Yes, Pete had certainly made his mark on the world. The notorious 'Hamlingate' episode had put him in the spotlight and propelled him to fame, but he had become somewhat bored of piping and wanted to shake off the naff stereotype. He dreamed of becoming an A-lister in his own right.

'There goes Pete Piper. He's so adorable, just look at his shiny teeth,' was what he longed to hear. Not 'There goes the smelly ratcatcher, keep smiling child-snatcher!'

An excited voice raced down the earpiece at lightening pace.

'Hey, slow down... KP! Long time, no hear.... A talent competition you say... and you want me to be a judge?' Pete wilted at the thought of spending anything more than a day in Evermore and continued to leaf through the pages of *Cosmetic Dentistry Today*. But something within the garbled message caught his attention.

'Hang on! did you say it's going to be on the telly? Now he was listening. His thoughts ran ahead of himself; Skyline TV, World Cable Network, his own chat show, Hollywood...

'OK, and there'll be no mention of the...you know,' he lowered his voice '...the rat thing?' He waited for confirmation.

'KP Dude, you just landed yourself a deal. Send the details to my secretary. Ciao bella!'

He lowered the phone back into its cradle, smoothed his hair and did a nifty shuffle towards the full-length mirror on the wall. Grabbing the stylish (if you like that kind of thing) frame with both hands he smiled seductively at his reflection.

'*YERSSSS*,' he breathed with a sultry snarl, 'who loves ya baby? This could be the lucky break we've been waiting for.' He gave himself a quick peck on the lips, snatched up the phone and began to dial.

'Tarquel, pack my bags and book a first-class ticket to Evermore, I'm going to be a STAAAR!'

'But Sir' Tarquel said, '*EVERMORE?*'

'I know,' said Pete, 'But that idiot King Pants thinks there's talent hiding in that backwards little Kingdom of his and, guess what? He wants me to find it! It'll be like trying to find pin head in a pigsty. And when I tell him there isn't any he's going to have to open the doors to *MEEE*...The Pied... I mean **Piper Music** and my International Stars. Evermore may be small and King Pants is definitely stupid, but he's richer than a weasel with gold teeth!' Pete let out a withering cackle.

WHOO-HA-HA-HA-HA

'Should I pack the flute Sir?' enquired the ever-loyal Tarquel.

'No, I won't be needing that old whistle this time. Get me some bands, the biggest, loudest, rockiest, dirtiest ones we have on the books. We're going to blow Evermore to pieces!'

'But what about the issue with the rats Sir, won't that be... er awkward?'

'That's in the past, Tarkers.'

'And Queen Rebobina?'

There was a small pause.

'Also history. Good Queen bloke! I can handle her. Now go book that flight, pack the bags and spread the word...

Evermore, HERE I COME!'

Chapter 7

The news is out!

Tarquel packed the flute anyway and booked the bands. Pretty soon news of the Evermore Talent Competition had spread quicker than a gassy bottom smell in a hot classroom. Everybody was talking about it… **all over the world!**

'I say old chap, have you heard that King Pants is having a talent competition in Evermore?'

'Well, I say that's marvellous what a laugh, everybody knows he won't find any! Ha ha ha ha!'

'Actung miene freunder, dat Kinky Pant ist doing der competer fur der talenter aust Evermore?'

'Dat ist de marvelousen mit um laughing, heer will nicht finden kleinen ist! Ha ha ha ha!'

'Eh gringo, molo Panty Kinko de competitio ollo talenti dias Evermore?'
'Donto marvelentio aventi laughibonto, donde de nono liberatio! Ha ha ha ha!'

'Ee em buto, do compo tonky Kinko Pantopant bom Evermore?'
'Duku wambo nob buko ebomby nubendi! Ha ha ha ha!'

And so on......

Chapter 8

Biscuits

'HUMPH! BLITHERING JAMJAM BLODGERS!'

Hilda the housekeeper slammed a rolling pin on the kitchen table.

WHACK!

The sudden noise caused a startled mouslet to choke on a handful of flour he was stealing. His friend poured some water down the throat of the asphyxiating sneak thief, but this just caused the flour to set like a concrete paste, creating a mouslet pasty with the crust on the inside.

At that moment Arthur Gardner the gardener poked his head round the kitchen door.

'Oy, Hilda? Any chance of a cup of tea and one of them luverly biscuits then?'

'HUMPH! Don't you go on talking to me about no biscuits Arthur. Costing me a fortune they is indeed, especially these blooming JamJammy blumin' Blodgers. It's a drain on me budget.' She plucked a pencil from her hair and ran her finger over the open page of the household ledger where she began to scribble.

'Well, how about these little beauties to cheer you up?' said Arthur, flinging a clump of soil-bedraggled beetradish onto the table.

'Arrrrthuur,' Hilda purred, shimmying her bustling skirts towards him and pinching his cheeks with her plump fingers, 'You know how to treat a lady. Sit yourself down then, I can spare five minutes.'

She plonked herself down on his knee like a dumpy bag full of saw dust landing on a pile of dried twigs.

'Ha-ha, that's my girl. So why do you keep buying these ...Hammy Rogers, why not bake your own?'

'Plodgers Arthur, JammyJam Dogbers!' Hilda chuckled, her robust frame shaking, causing the stool legs to rattle. 'Because her ladyship keeps ordering 'em that's why and we can't just make them here, we haven't got the quickment. They must use some sort of machine to make the little heart shape in the middle and the fiddly pattern on top.'

'Well, I reckons your homemade sweetmeats takes some beating,' said Arthur, carefully concealing a wince, for it took a strong man to bear the full weight of Hilda the Housekeeper, especially when she started jiggling around a bit which she did when she started to get giddy (and Arthur did tend to have that effect on her).

Nonetheless she didn't seem to mind when their downtime was cut short, for Hilda found herself pleasantly distracted by a curious notion that Arthur had planted in her mind – unwittingly introducing a new thread that will weave seamlessly into our plot.

Chapter 9

Lights, Camera, Action

'AND NOW! a great voice boomed.
LIVE,
it boomed again,
THE STAR OF THE SHOW,
BOOM
THE ONE AND ONLY, YOUR VERY OWN
BOOM, BOOM, BOOM

KIIIIIIING.....PANTS!!!'

The curtains swooshed open, the King was blinded by a thousand spotlights, cameras beamed the image to every TV in the known multiverse. Everyone who lived, had lived or had even heard of Evermore sat encased in plush velvet chairs staring at him.........in stunned silence.

King Pants peered out into the crowd, squinting so hard his nostrils hovered above his eyes. The Queen sat in the front row next to the biggest set of perfect shiny teeth. Pete Piper was grinning from ear to there.

'Kiiing PANTS wears silly old PANTS
And Silly old PANTS says he!'

The chanted rhyme sounded menacing and sinister,
especially when followed by a most irreverent, slow-mocking
hand clap…

'HE AIN' T GOT A CHANCE!
OF GOING TO THE DANCE!'

Pete Piper stood up and hollered to the crowd,

'CAN' T DANCE – NO CHANCE!' went the variation on a
theme.

The auditorium exploded with laughter.

The air became thick like a suffocating blanket and the
chanting lips of the crowd merged into one singular mouth
which moved closer towards the quivering King and seemed
to swell in size until it threatened to engulf him entirely. His
ears went numb with terror and hid behind his head.

NO CHANCE! NO PANTS!

CLAP, CLAP.

A fresh burst of laughter erupted in slow motion when a
small boy stood up and pointed. 'Look!'

Everyone fell about laughing. They doubled up with
hysterics, holding their bellies. Some cheered, some hid their
eyes, some covered their gaping mouths, some took
photographs. One man even did a quick sketch, but it wasn't
very good.

After looking around everywhere it finally dawned on the
King that they were laughing and pointing at him. Glancing
down he realised why.

He was absolutely, totally and utterly, beyond a shadow of doubt, pork sausage NAKED!

'WHAAAAAAAAAAAAAAAAAAAAAAAAA AAH!' he screamed as he shot bolt upright in bed.

A driplet of freezing cold sweat ran down his back and headed for a gap between his skin and pyjama bottoms.

'Oooooh!' he cried as it found its target.

'What am I doing?' the King gibbered, remembering the nightmarish dream. 'Am I mad?'

'Quite possibly,' remarked a bleary eyed Aspinol, annoyed at being awakened from a lovely dream where he was running wild and free, barefoot through the burning hot sands of his childhood Savanna.

'"You?...what...where's the Queen?' King Pants sat upright in a puddle of cold sweat and confusion.

'She has of late become involved in the concept and fabrication of her attire for the forthcoming spectacular,' informed the sleepy ostrich.

'Eh?'

'She's making her outfit for the big night,' quipped Aspinol turning over and nicking half the duvet.

'Oh!'

The befuddled monarch sank back into his soggy pit and still, somewhat troubled, drifted off into a deepless sleep...

'*AND NOW...*' boomed a great voice....

Chapter 10

Evermore gets ready...nearly

'HUMPH!'

Hilda the Housekeeper cruised down the Castle corridor like expanding treacle. Cat the mousleteer, blissfully unaware of how close he had just been to becoming a Filthy Lurker's evening meal, was sleeping on a rug happily digesting a couple of pastry-filled mouslets when he became engulfed in Hilda's vast folds, wiping the satisfied smile right off his smug face.

'HUMPH!'

In her oversized hands Hilda carried an oversize tray of suspicious looking overfilled sandwiches, jammy biscuits and mugs of luke-cold tea. Following her closely and carrying an equal supply of provisions scampered Betty Botter the new maid.

'Phew, it isn't half hard work and all this carrying these great big and heavy great plates so it is not that I'm complaining at all so I am not because as you know I am ever so grateful so I am for getting this job and letting me work in the Castle and learn how to make sarnies and tea which I'm sure is a wonderful skill and all that so it is,' chattered Betty tirelessly.

'HUMPH!' continued Hilda. She was not at all happy.

'Up and down, up and down. More sarnies, more tea, any sugar? Shall I stir it with mi spare big toe?' she grumbled sarcastically.

The Castle was overrun with 'Roadies' from the **ΣBC** (Evermore Broadcasting Company), grubby men in grubby t-shirts carrying cables, cameras, lights and boxes who consumed mountains of sarnies and gallons of tea.

They wore faded, dirty, jeans that exposed large hairy bottoms areas when they bent over, which was quite often it seemed.

'The first time I saw one I thought it was a Filthy Lurker with a centre parting and tried to kick it out of the way.' Hilda grumbled to Betty the maid. 'I mean it's not hygienic. And I wish they'd stop shouting **HUMPH!**'

'Up here! Over there!' the men shouted 'Down there! In here! To me! To you! More tea! More sarnies! **HUMPH!**

'OY! WHO THREW THAT?!' A large, tattooed and particularly sweaty man pulled an ice cube out from between his hairy bum cheeks. Inside the Castle the Queen and Aspinol hid behind the curtains, giggling like a pair of childish mouslets.

'This is a great game, Asp!' snorted the Queen. 'Go get some more ice.'

'Your wish is my command O' Great Ice Queen!' Aspinol scurried off, his ability to scurry somewhat impaired by the fact that he was trying so hard not to laugh he had to cross his long skinny legs.

'Can't you two do that quietly or better still in silence or even better somewhere else completely?' complained the King as he plumped an opulent, golden, royal crest-emblazened cushion. 'I didn't get a wink of sleep last night.'

He was trying desperately to relax by watching reruns of his favourite TV programme **Dealest Thou or Dealest Thou Not** presented by that master of the pernicious pun Noddy Oddbod.

'Awwwh, didn't the Kingy Wingy get to sleepy weepy last nighty wighty?' mocked Queen Bob as she took careful aim once again with a fresh batch of frozen ammunition 'Who's fault is that then?'

'Well, Quazimodo have you got a HUNCH what could be in the next box?' droned the telly.

'After all, you started all this with your daft idea,' she started to mimic the King: '*I want some new music. Hey, let's have a talent competition. Let's televise it to the whole world. Let's invite some prancing shiny-toothed* **IDIOT***!!!'*

'Actually, I think that was my idea, Ma'am,' Aspinol interjected. 'Obviously not the prancing shiny-toothed idiot element.'

King Pants pushed his fingers deep into his ears. Inside his head was much nicer. He was swimming with calm fishes and tranquil terrapins dancing effortless somersaults in a warm waveless sea.

'Well, Quazi does this RING ANY BELLS?' the telly persevered.

King Pants could see Noddy's lips move but just for a moment everything in his world was unspoilt....until an ice cube crashed into the back of his head.

'DEAL!' shouted Quazimodo.

'DING DONG!' shouted Noddy Oddbod.

'OOOW!' shouted the King.

'*ARE YOU LISTENING TO ME?*' shouted the Queen.

'Excellent shot,' whispered Aspinol.

Being blessed with innate charm as he was and looking so vulnerable sitting with his poor bruised and still chilly head in a cushion whimpering softly, it would have been impossible for anyone with half a heart to be angry with King Pants for long.

'This is what you wanted, remember? Don't worry sweetie, it's going to be great,' soothed a tender voice.

'Shut up Aspinol,' butted in Queen Bob. 'Eddie, get a grip and get real. It'll probably be rubbish, but hey, it'll be a laugh. What time's the toothy fairy turning up anyway?'

'I rang him earlier,' the King sighed, his self-esteem now lower than a worm's belly button. 'His secretary Caio Bella, said he'd already left for the airport, but I could 'eye message' him, whatever that means, on his phone if I had an apple. I told her I had loads... an orchard full of them. I think she were impressed.'

King Pants still wasn't entirely sure why he'd been asked that question. Was there a shortage of apples in the rest of the world? Why would Pete have only one? He shrugged, surrendering defeat.

'I better get ready to meet him, I suppose.'

'Er, aren't you going to get change out of *those*!' exclaimed the Queen. Her eyes did that pointy downwards thing.

The King's eyes followed and tried, in vain, to focus on the multi-coloured vomit-inducing leg ornaments he was wearing. 'My pants?' he enquired.

Queen Bob and Aspinol both nodded in agreement, exchanging knowing looks.

'Exactly' said the Queen. 'They're so **PANTS!**'

Chapter 11

Oooh You're a fat one!

You knows wat I finks fellas' said a fat Filthy Lurker 'I finks we's gonna right like it 'ere. Ee's a gud un that bloke, even if ee's gots a nose likes a dogs.'

The recently unemployed dog-nosed Eudar seller walked up and down between the rows of tightly packed cages. Each was full of Filthy Lurkers of all shapes and sizes from fat to very fat. Every so often he would stop to glance a beady bloodshot eye into one of the steel mesh pens. 'Ooooh! You're a fat one,' he would say rubbing his hands together.

'Thanks you muchly,' replied the Filthy Lurker 'Yes me brovers thises the life. We got us own rooms and loads o' this green stuffs t' eats. Beet's tryin' to catch a sneaky mouslet in a dark smelly corridor. I even 'ad a baff 'ont way in.'

'But where d'y finks ees takin' that lot?' A smaller, younger Filthy Lurker pointed to Dognose picking up cages and carrying them off.

'Them's is lucky un's, them's gettin' wot's called an upgrade. Wen ee opens that door the smell o' food is 'eavenly. If you's eats y' green stuff an' get's fatted up you's'll be goin' in there's too.'

'More fat ones, Simon!' Dognose chucked some more cages through the door marked

PIE KITCHEN

The smell that came out was indeed heavenly.

Simple Simon picked up the cages and took them through to the Pieman.
Simple Simon had met the Pieman going to the fair.
Simple Simon had said to the Pieman 'Can I taste you wares?'
'No!' said the Pieman 'Oi ain't got any, 'aven't you 'erd all dem Eudars 'ave taked der laws into their own 'ands and run orf someplace, hoo knows wheres?'
Simple Simon had a little think, hatched a little plan, did some sums, came up with a bright idea and right there and then the FILLET LE CARRE PIE CO was created.
Simple Simon then met the Piperman, on the telephone.
The Piperman to simple Simon said 'Can I buy your shares?'
Simple Simon said to the Piperman 'I'm not sure what shares are, but I am more than happy to sell them.'
Right there and then Peter Piper arranged to buy the FILLET LE CARRE PIE CO for cash with his new business partner.

'Not so simple now.' Simon congratulated himself in the morning as he awoke inside the wardrobe with his shoes tied to his head.

Chapter 12

The Piper rides in

Alarge crowd of about five unemployed market traders and some children had been paid to wave flags and cheer the arrival of the Piper.

King Pants and his Queen stood with noble dignity on the Great Staircase leading to the Great Doors of the Castle.

'I wish he'd get a wriggle on,' whispered Queen Bob 'This standing with noble dignity is making my knickers dig in!'

Finally, the entourage pulled up on the Great Driveway.

'What a loathsome bunch of peasants,' remarked Pete to Tarquel through an enforced beam of a smile 'If they were any more backwards they'd be on all fours.'

Tarquel stared at the raggedy crowd through the window.

'And as for King Pants standing there like some sort of regal scarecrow. Whatever did Queen Bob see in him? When she could have had..'

'You, Sir?'

'It all. She could have had it all.'

'Remember why you're here, Sir,' chided the rather sensible and ever-loyal PR.

'Oh! I know why I'm here Tarkers baby.' Pete was suddenly serious (and a little bit scarily dramatic). 'I *know* why I'm here.'

'Here he is,' hissed the Queen sideways through her gritted smile. 'Same as ever, preened to perfection and as slippery as a lubricated oil slick on ice.'

'Now now Queenie, be nice.' The King stepped forward with arms outstretched like a kindly father welcoming a long lost son.

'Don't do that Eddie it makes you look like a scarecrow,' nudged Queen Bob.

'Thank you, thank you.' Pete smiled, waved and bowed for his adoring fans as he stepped down from the coach.

'*Booooooo!*' cheered the crowd and ran off laughing, waving their ill-gotten gains.

'I knew I should have paid them when they'd finished,' groaned the soon-to-be-sacked crowd organizer.

'It's like coming home.' Pete told the reporters as he posed for photos with the King and Queen on the Great Steps. '*THIS* is going to be the biggest thing ever to hit Evermore.'
FLASH!
'Apart from when the Giant fell down the Beanstalk!' He paused for a laugh that never came.
FLASH!
'My friends!' He hugged the King and Queen, giving ostentatious air kisses, and grinning for the lens.
FLASH!
'Never fear - **Piper Music** is here! Let's go find us some talent.' A few more full-length photos of Pete by himself.

FLASH!

FLASH!

FLASH!

Then the reporters and photographers were shooed away before King Pants had chance to read his welcome speech.

'Right KP, Let's go!' Pete Piper put his arm around the slightly stunned King and frogmarched him away from the cameras. 'No time to lose, we've got work to do.'

Off they whooshed leaving the Queen and Aspinol staring at the backs of the Piper entourage. They looked at each other, speechless and a bit embarrassed.

'First, here's my contract and my list of things we need.' Pete thrust a huge wad of paper into the King's bewildered hands. 'Next, let's get you down to wardrobe. Then it's hair, walkthrough, rehearsal, after-party rehearsal, make-up, teeth whitening, posing and smiling practice, sarcastic comment writing workshop, spray tan...' The King's head began to spin. He glanced down to check if his feet were still actually touching the ground as they sped along the corridor. Pete's monologue continued racing at tireless pace.

'...dressing rooms, food, chairs, total control and...' Peter paused and pulled the King close to hiss in his ear.

'*Who's the tall, skinny guy with the Queen?*'

'That's Aspinol.' replied King Pants happy that he had finally understood something that Pete had said. 'He's an ostrich.'

'I don't care where he's from I just don't trust him. His eyes are like, too..'

'Close together?' suggested Tarquel.

'High up?' called the make-up lady.

'Occular?' proposed the script writing team.

'Boiled eggs!' said King Pants. Everybody stopped to look at him.

'His eyes are like two boiled eggs!' The King repeated, feeling rather pleased with himself at finding the most suitable simile.

Pete rolled his eyes and sighed. 'Come on. No time to lose. We really have a LOT of work to do!'

And off they all went at high speed again.

'Have you seen the King?' the Queen asked a servant sometime later.

'I think his Majesty and the Piper are in the great ballroom Ma'am,' came the reply.

'Have you seen the King?' the Queen asked a cleaner.

'A seen 'im wit' Ratman, they went that way.'

'Have you seen the King?' the Queen asked the clod-scrapers apprentice.

'Arrrrrrrrrrr King aye I aseen, stinkin' rat teeth eeeeeeeeeeee shineee arrrh!'

'Hilda, have you seen the King?'

'HUMPH, I've seen him alright and if you ask me he's making a fool of himself hanging out with that smelly rat wrangler who in my opinion is making a fool of him too and this whole thing if you want to know what I think I'll tell you and as for making more sarnies and tea, up and down, up and down.'

'I'm bored Aspinol,' she confided 'It's no fun without Eddie. I haven't seen anything of him since *THAT* Piper arrived.'

'Very well, you can always annoy me if you want,' offered her fine feathered friend.

She tried punching the ostrich in the leg, but it wasn't the same.

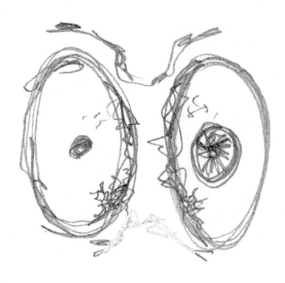

Chapter 13

It's Showtime!

And then it happened, it finally happened. The stage was set, the cameras were ready, the audience were seated, an owl hooted in the night sky and somewhere in a distant desert a cactus plant died, but never mind it had lived a long and relatively happy life. King Pants looked down to double check he was wearing clothes and took a deep nervous gulp of air.

'AND NOW!' a great voice boomed.

'LIVE,' it boomed again. King Pants started to feel hot and sweaty. He loosened his leopard-print bow tie.

'FOR THE FIRST TIME EVER,'
BOOM
'WELCOME TO...'

BOOM
BOOM

'EVERMORE'S..'

BOOM

'GOT..'

BOOM

'TALENT!'

Jack Sprat sprung onto the stage like a daddy-long-legs in a catsuit, smiling and waving. His wife Jaqueline on the other hand was being helped up by four strong men with a hydraulic pump and a dumper truck.

'Welcome to **EVERMORE'S GOT TALENT!**' puffed Jaqueline. The audience clapped, stamped their feet, howled and cheered. The ones at the back made rude noises with their armpits and twanged elastic bands. Then Jack took over while Jaqueline went for a sit down.

'Let's meet our fabulous judging panel. First the Queen of all our hearts, Queen Rebobina.'

The Queen stood up and waved excitedly, showing off her new dress and quite a bit more. The entire creation was made from red silk hearts barely (and I mean barely) held together with large safety pins. The crowd went wild. There was even a wolf whistle, followed by a single blast as a woodsman shot the wolf, which raised a huge cheer from a coach load of pigs from out of town.

'Wooooooweeeeeeee!' beamed Jack, resisting the urge to whistle. 'Look at you! you look amazing. WOW! just look, doesn't she look amazing everyone?' The crowd cheered again in agreement. 'Wow, Queen Rebobina, amazing, just look, WOW!'

'That's enough looking...Jack!' Jaqueline scowled as she struggled to her feet.

'Sit down Bob,' urged King Pants with a mixed feeling of admiration and unusual possessiveness. 'You'll give the idiot a heart attack.'

Jaqueline poked her gibbering spouse in the ribs.

'Next,' continued Jack Sprat, reading the inside of his palm, 'The man who made it all possible, without who's ingee, ingeeny...'

'Ingenious!' prompted Jacqueline behind a pretend cough.

'Ingenious inspiration this show would not exist. Our very own beloved...'

King Pants blushed slightly and pushed back his chair ready to stand up.

'...PETER PIPER!'

He watched hopelessly as Pete rose majestically right on cue.

The hyped-up crowd went wild. Pete flashed his Hollywood teeth, bowed to the audience with a flourish, a twirl, a smile and a prance and a sideways saucy wink to Jaqueline Sprat.

Blushing, Jacqueline took the microphone and tapped it a few times, sending the sound crew reeling as they battled with the feedback.

'And finally, His Majesty, King Pan.. whoops, sorry, I mean Edgar. King Edgar.' Still feeling crestfallen, King Pants remained seated despite receiving an air kiss from Jacqueline and a round of applause from Queen Bob.

'EVERMORE'S GOT TALENT is sponsored by THE FILLET LE CARRE PIE CO. Talent topped with egg glazed shortcrust,' continued Jaqueline, licking her lips. 'Now, on with the show.'

The Stage darkened to a single spotlight, the audience held its breath. All was silent until somebody dropped a massive pin, which made an awful din. The curtain twitched, a weak coughing sound could be heard, followed by a tap-tap-tapping as a little grey-haired man, bent almost double, hobbled onto the stage. He stood in the spotlight, wheezing.

'What's your name?' asked Pete with a look of bewilderment.

'I'm the crooked man,'

'And where do you come from?'

'The crooked house.'

'And did you come far to be here tonight?'

'I walked a crooked mile and crossed a crooked stile.'

For a second Pete's immaculate smile wavered.

'Is this some kind of a joke?' he whispered to Queen Bob.

'No that is the crooked man, he's been around for ages, he's got a huge following,' the Queen whispered back.

'Following? The only place you could follow this old codger is the graveyard!'

The Queen snorted into her glass of water.

Then the audience gasped audibly as the crooked man launched into a chorus of This Old House, shuffling and twisting, badly out of time. His screeching voice sounded like a flamingo in a flour sack being mauled by a large wheezy bear. Eventually he stopped singing altogether to catch his breath and steady his balance. As he staggered towards the second chorus a clutch of paramedics rushed onto the stage bearing a stretcher.

The cameras immediately swung to the judging panel.

44

ZOOM   Big close up of King Pants.

    ZOOM

      ZOOM

         ZOOM

– three different angle shots of Queen Rebobina's safety pins. Even Pete Piper was starting to feel upstaged by *that* dress.

'*Err*..well,' began the King. 'Bravo. A bit shaky in the middle, but you really carried it off at the end. Boom-boom! Carried it off.... get it?' There was silence in the auditorium. Someone coughed awkwardly.

'It's a no from me. Sorry.' he said glumly.

'It was HILARIOUS!' hooted Queen Bob, clapping her hands with glee, 'YES, YES, YES!'

Then it was Pete Piper's turn.

'That was the worst act I have ever seen. It was like watching a bandy-legged frog being electrocuted while being forced to gargle with cotton wool wrapped in barbed wire. So, well it's obviously a

NO!

NO!

NO!'

Pete Piper hammered the words with his fist to howls of laughter.

The Three Blind Mice were up next. At least it can't get any worse, thought the little girl in the second from the front row before things got even worse. At least there's no nasty screeching that will hurt my ears, thought the sweet little granny sitting by her side before the screeching started. The visually impaired rodents danced around giddily till eventually one of them fell off the stage and into the orchestra pit.

Eeeeeeek! screeched a lady violinist.

The second (who was the first mouse's cousin) fell down the bell of a trombone.

Squeeeeeek! screeched the mouse.

The third who was the first mouse's sister, also a cousin of the second mouse, knocked over part of the set (a giant polystyrene piece of cheese – how could she possibly not see that!).

Bleeeep! screeched the set-builder.

King Pants buried his head in his hands. This was all a big mistake. It would end in tears - he could feel it in his loins (whatever they were). Pete Piper stroked his smile with a mean finger. This was the best thing ever - he could feel it in his silken slippers. Daring to glance up again, the King stared aghast as a hysterical OAP waving a snapped violin screamed all the way to the exit. Queen Bob was laughing so much her silk hearts were beginning split.

ZOOM

ZOOM   *refocus*

ZOOM!!!!

Poor King Pants. Surely there had to be some talent somewhere in Evermore. But, alas, Tom Thumb could hardly be seen never mind heard.

'Can't you stand on a box?' called Pete Piper.

'I am standing on a box,' came the feeble reply.

'That's three no's from me,' decreed King Pants (a funny line he thought up all by himself).

'*Imbecile!*' muttered the snide Piper.

Meanwhile the Queen was running out of oxygen, so Aspinol had to deliver the bad news on her behalf.

'I'm afraid it's another no,' he said sympathetically.

Lucy Locket sang a lovely song all about lovely things that grow in lovely gardens and how lovely everything was. She had obviously practised very hard and picked her lovely outfit very carefully and the whole thing was just lovely.

She still got two rejections. Only Queen Bob gave her a thumbs up.

'Lovely.' said Jack. 'And now Little Boy Blue.'

Little Boy Blue tooted a trio of traditional tunes but failed to impress.

'Sure, he can play the trumpet, but the name and that outfit and his choice of material - all wrong.' Slicing the air with his hand Peter Piper rolled his eyes. 'He comes across like some kind of... I don't know... backwards bugle-blowing farmyard animal entertainer in baggy breeches.'

'*NO!*'
'*NO!*'
'*NO!*'

Bring on the next lot. Surely things can only get better, thought the audience collectively.

But, alas, Old Mother Hubbard's half-starved dog was doing some great tricks until he fainted from hunger and the paramedics had to be rushed on again.

Solomon Grundy had to cancel because it was a Saturday. Although he was kind enough to invite everyone to his christening on Tuesday and his wedding on Wednesday as usual.

And Tommy Tucker wouldn't sing until he was fed.

'NO!'
'NO!'
'NO!'

They came, they performed, and they flopped like undercooked pancakes. The audience became restless and started to boo and jeer. Jack Sprat saved the day by running on and calling an advert break, but not before a quick plug for THE FILLET LE CARRE PIE CO.

'Gravy that's never out of tune,' he grinned with a cheery wave.

Exit stage left.

Chapter 14

At the Fillet le Carre Pie Co.

Unit. 13B Back Street, Evermore. EV1 3DD

In the back kitchen bit, by the gloom of a cooling oven sat three shady characters. They stared silently for quite a long time at a huge mound of cash. It was arranged carefully in a cash-shaped mound on the dirty blood-soaked table in front of their staring eyes. They would have continued to sit and stare in silence for quite a while longer had not one of them spoken.

'Whats did you say 'is name was 'gen?' asked the Pieman as he wiped a bogey on his grimy apron.

"Peter. Peter Piper," answered Simple Simon.

'Peter Peter Piper?'

'No just Peter.'

'Not Piper?'

'Yes Piper... Peter Piper.'

'Piper Peter Piper?'

'No! just P-e-t-e-r-P-i-p-e-r.' Simon reiterated.

'And why exactly did P-e-t-e-r-P-i-p-e-r give us all this money?'

'He said it was to secure sole rights to THE FILLET LE CARRE PIE CO branding and unique secret recipe along with a 99.9% share in the net and gross profits for the foreseeable fiscal future.'

'What?'

Simon shrugged.

'An whats we get out of it, all this making lots o' pies? Oi's med more pies in't last two days than Oi's ever med in mi entire life.'

'Yes well, he also said he would ensure worldwide advertising coverage, job security and lots more cash,' added Simon smugly. 'So, you'd better both get that oven fired up, you're going to be really busy.'

'An whats on this earth do all that mean?' asked the Pieman.

'Lots more cash, that's the only bit I got,' admitted Simon.

'Oi finks its an aw core blimey lets leggit trap,' said the third man who had yet to speak but just did. He was of course our old friend Dognose, and these three gentlemen were the collective workforce of THE FILLET LE CARRE PIE CO, if you hadn't already guessed.

'Do 'em know what's it is we's is doin's 'ere?' asked the Pieman wiping a bogey on his grimy apron. 'Oi mean's Oi does it and even Oi know's it be despicables.'

'Of course they do,' assured Simon. 'The fella with the big teeth says he can get us as many Filthy Lurkers as we want, says he can round 'em up just by whistling.'

'Oi still finks it be a sneeky let's be 'avin yous trap!' butts in Dognose.

'Of course, it's not a trap!' exclaimed Simon.

'Whys ain't it?'

'Because if it was a trap, my canine-nuzzled cohort, you would be behind bars hanging from a rope upside down,' Simon tried to reassure his accomplice.

Through the greasy walls echoed the sound of hundreds of Filthy Lurkers as they chatted amongst themselves, singing, eating and farting, (filthy Lurker farts are notoriously loud.)

'Whats ee look like this ere fella then?' asked the Pieman wiping a bogey on his grimy apron.

'He looked at bit like that ratcatcher bloke, big shiny teeth... molars like man traps.'

'Told yers there wers a trap!' butted in Dognose.

'There was another bloke with him looked a bit like King Pants all mad hair and a funny little crown,' continued Simon, ignoring his companion.

'Ha!' cracked the Pieman, rocking on his stool and wiping a bogey on his grimy apron, 'As if 't King and Pied Piper would pop in ere an' drop us off a load o' moneys! That be t'funniest fink Oi finks Oi's ever 'ad in me ears!'

When they had all stopped laughing at the thought of a royal visit, the Pieman returned to the matter in hand.

'Did yer signs owt?'

'Yes of course I signed something,' Simon went on.

'Wot dis yer sign?' asked the Pieman wiping a bogey on his grimy apron.

'Your name.'

'You simple or what?'

'Right! It's late I'm off to watch that *EVERMORE'S GOT TALENT* thing that everyone's banging on about,' said

Simon, clapping his hands and rubbing them together. 'What are we going to do with all this money? We can't leave it here, on account of the fact that I don't trust you two villains. So, I'll take half for doing all the negotiating and stuff.'

'Alright me an Dognose gonna take the other two halfs,' suggested the Pieman wiping a bogey on his grimy apron.

'Oy! Yous cheaters!' chipped in Dognose, 'If yous gettin arf an' ees gettin arf an' Oi's avin arf ....'

'Yes,'

'Who's gets the uver 'arf?'

'!'

Chapter 15

During the adverts

' IT'S A DISASTER ! '

Cried King Pants bristling and bustling into the dressing room.

'It's *your* disaster!' retorted Pete 'You'll be lucky if you get out of here alive, that ugly mob could turn nasty - let's face it they couldn't turn any uglier.' The Piper hid a sneaky snigger behind his lanolined palm.

'What are we going to do?'

'I have no idea what YOU are going to do, my Sovereign, I'm off to make a phone call.' Pete promptly swished out of the room like an expensive curtain.

'Ah Tunaduck and Caulicumber sandwiches,' cried Queen Bob diving into the hospitality nosh.

'It was BRILLIANT!' she declared spinning round and spitting crumbs everywhere. 'Got any booze?'

'These sarnies are ace, I'm dying for a wee.' And off she dashed nearly stampeding the director who was just entering the room.

The King looked at Louie Marcello Bontenostrumienotto and tried in vain to rack his perforated memory. Now what was his name?

'King Edgar!' The director announced with a flouncy air kiss.

That's it...King Edgar! The King was relieved he hadn't forgotten after all.

'Izza pure genioso! Brillianto! Magnafico!' Louie Marcello Bontenostrumienotto declared in a thinly disguised Irish accent.

'You ara so funny Mr King the audience they alla love you. They Alla love La Bella Queenie Rebobina!' He nudged King Pants with his elbow and winked. 'She'sa one a hota mama eh, witha the dress anda legs anda hips anda...'

SLAM!

Pete burst into the room with a dramatic shriek.

'Anda you!' Louie Marcello Bontenostrumienotto turned his attention to the Piper 'You are soa incredibly RUDE. ABOMINABLY RUDE! But what is zis? Ze camrah is not shooting nowa. You musta relax a bit, stoppa being a, how you say, so upa tight ass!'

'Genioso! Brillianto! Magnafico!' The director declared again.

Pete was still blushing as the great Louie Marcello Bontenostrumienotto swooped out of the room.

'Well,' said King Pants 'I don't think he was very happy!'

'Are you joking?' Pete squeaked. Then he cleared his throat and spoke as clearly as an over excited banjo bouncing down a fire escape. 'I've just spoken to the TV Exec and ratings are up 200% with pie sales up 800% and rising! This is the biggest thing ever!' And off he swished again with a flamboyant swirl of his hips.

'Tarquel, get Simon. We need more pies!'

'Hello gorgeous.' The Queen came back into the room still trying to tuck herself back into her dress (which was not easy as she'd had to undo twenty-two safety pins just to go to the toilet.) King Pants was sucking thoughtfully on the damp corner of a featureless imitation bread snack product. He looked up to see who Queen Bob was talking to.

'Give us a hand here Eddie,' she said, tugging at the stretchy fabric.

The King dropped his sandwich onto his shoe and with trembling fingers helped the Queen secure her dignity behind a few well-placed silken hearts. He couldn't remember a time someone ever had such an effect on him.

'Wow - you're looking hot,' she said teasing his hair with her fingers. 'Very Rock and Roll. I do like a man in leather pants.'

King Pants blushed, his heart pounding like a frenzied ferret in a cheap suitcase. He thought it might be a good time to say something nice, a compliment, an admiring comment or flattering remark. His eyes glazed over, and he could feel a bit of dribble forming in the corner of his mouth.

The Queen stepped back and did a twirl holding her hands in the air. The King nearly fainted as the blood rushed from his head.

'So? What do you think?'

'C..c..cool...shoes,' he muttered, when his tongue finally prised itself off the roof of his mouth.

'And?'

Why was he acting like someone who couldn't talk?

'You, you look........nice.' The words came out as sweetly and smoothly as warm honey.

'Hey, Eddie…..' it was the Queen's turn to be lost for words.

The two of them stood in silence, feeling awkward.

'Oy, you two - get a move on!' A grumpy roadie called through the door. He had been in a bad mood ever since that curious and still yet unexplained incident with an ice cube, which had caused a mysterious and very irritable rash to appear between his clammy buttocks. 'One minute to camera.'

'Right! I'm off!' announced the Queen 'I've got things to do, be back at the end of the show!'

'*What?*' whimpered King Pants 'Things? What things?'

'A Surprise!' replied Queen Bob.

The hairy roadie burst into the room and grabbed the King by the ear dragging him back to his chair.

Queen Bob was already gone.

Chapter 16

The Whole World's Watching, the Whole World's Watching

All over the world televisions were tuned to the *EBC* channel. In some countries it was very early in the morning and in others it was well past bedtime, and that's to do with the way the Sun travels all the way round the Earth every couple of days and all that.

Eager viewers literally glued themselves to their chairs so as not to miss the second half. Some of them had missed the first half and were so busy talking about missing it they were probably going to miss the second half as well. Even people who didn't have televisions stared into the corner of a room and pretended they did.

'Oooh! Look it's our Mary Mary!' shouted Mrs Contrary waving at the screen 'Coooeee Mary Mary. Aw, 'aint she sweet.'

'No, she's not sweet, she's bonny,' called back Mr Contrary.

'Bonny? Mary Mary's not bonny. She's sweet.'

'Sweet? Mary Mary's not sweet, she's bonny.' And so the bickering continued all the way through their daughter's performance.

'Has she finished?'

'Who?'

'Did we miss it?'

'I'm sure I've seen those two judges before,' muttered Simple Simon to a broken light bulb he had just made friends with.

All over the planet people were talking about the show.

'I say some of these Evermore chaps and chapesses are ever so good.' A posh chap remarked to his posh acquaintances. 'I particularly appreciate the fine skills and artistry of Little Jack Horner. Did you witness the delicate extraction? An exquisite example of a Prunus Gage using only his Digitus Primus, I say. Bravo!'

In another part of the world

'Wells oy never. Thats bloke just pulled out a plum with is thumb!'

'I just know I've seen those two before Mr Bulbhead,' said Simon. He had given his new friend a name.

'I likee her, she sing vely nice song.'
'Who you likee?'
'I likee lady who sing song I likee.'
'I likee too.'

'Have you ever seen them before, Mr Bulbhead? I have. I'm sure I have.'

'How come we don't got this show?' The Chairman of WWTVCN (World Wide TV Channel Network) barked at his sycophantic staff. 'It's a work of genius, this *EVERMORE'S GOT TALENT.* This is what the masses want to watch. It's real, it's funny, it's got heart... this is life, people. And you're all fired!' He slammed his fist hard down on the polished boardroom table, just to make everyone jump (making people jump was his favourite thing).

'Now Mr Bulbhead we haven't known each other very long, but I feel I can trust you and I hope you feel the same. So, if you do have an inkling as to who these two men are I would very much like you to tell me. You can whisper it if you want, or just write it down on a piece of paper if that would make it easier.'
Mr Bulbhead said nothing.

All over the planet everyone was talking about who they wanted to win.

'Who d'y think'll win?'

'Oy wudst be loiken that Mess Murfet t' win.'

'Nonono she' um fraid um Spider that um nono.'

'Ich canicht warten to finden oust.'

' MAYBEES LA QUEEN.. SHE HEFA DA TALENTS...YES? '

Simon had Mr Bulbhead tied to a chair. 'Now you fiend, you've got information, I just know it, and I'm going to make you talk. You tell me who these men are or I'll.....'

'Alright I'll talk!' Mr Bulbhead finally cracked under the pressure (which seems a bit harsh as he was already blown). 'It's King Pants and the Pied Piper - the same men who came to your pie factory a few days ago and gave you all that money.'

'So *THAT'S* who it is! O.K. That wasn't difficult was it?' said Simon untying the sobbing bulb. 'You're free to go, but don't leave town. I may have to ask you some more questions.'

'He's not very bright,' thought the broken lightbulb.

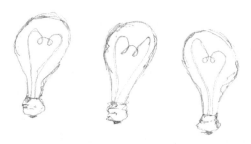

'Can I go on *EVERMORE'S GOT TALENT* Mum?' A little boy asked his tired but adoring Mother.

'Well, I don't know, maybe.'

'Pleeeeaase let me go on *EVERMORE'S GOT TALENT,* Mum.'

'But what would you do Darling?'

The little boy put his head on one side and thought for a while.

'I can blow smelly bubbles in the bath,' he declared with pride.

Chapter 17

The second half of the Show! (and the Queen's Surprise)

'Welcome back ladies and gentlemen and you lot up there in the cheap seats,' hailed Jack as the cameras whirred into focus.

'I hope you had time to enjoy a FILLET LE CARRE pie during the break,' called Jaqueline. 'I had four,' she said and slumped back into a special seat that had been installed.

Then she hiccupped and promptly fell asleep, missing the rest of the show.

The following hour was just a cavalcade of misery, awfulness, pie adverts, meaningless nonsense and endless mediocrity. Act after act came, performed, crashed and burned in a bonfire of ear-wetting tonsil-twisting vocals and eye-cringing dance moves. The best being only slightly better than the worst and the worst only slightly better than watching something rubbish being performed badly by a talentless binbag.

The final act, Barry Binbag, slowly walked off the stage to roars of *'Rubbish!'*

'Well, there we have it, folks. You've now seen all the acts, and the judges have made their decision.' Jack spoke down the lens of camera three with all the earnestness of a politician who was launching a campaign against cruelty to custard. 'It appears that a grand total of no acts at all have made it through to the grand final.'

'None, zero, ziltch, nada, nought, diddly squat, goose egg, nix!' He swivelled towards the judging panel.

'Why is that Your Majesty?'

King Pants was weeping inconsolably into a Caulicumber sandwich and couldn't speak.

'Peter?' asked Jack.

Pete Piper leaned back in his chair chewing the end of his pen, and pausing deliberately, enjoying the moment. He waved the pen at Jack with a slow wrist, like a hitman taking aim with his deadliest weapon.

Leaning dramatically towards the microphone he hesitated to allowed himself another dramatic pause, for the drama.

'It appears that Evermore *hasn't* got talent!' he said eventually.

The crowd was silent. He let the words sink in.

He looked out into the audience, at a sea of gaping mouths, transfixed on him, enchanted. Pride got the better of him. He could feel it swelling up inside like a balloon being filled with power, money, opportunity and more money.

Then he spoke again. 'Yet… that may not be *entirely* true,' he added. 'Evermore does have a talent for making pies, especially THE FILLET LE CARRE PIE CO.'

(Big smile to camera One).

The audience nodded in agreement as free pie tokens were handed out.

'But!' The Piper snapped 'Musically… no talent whatsoever!'

The King blew his nose. He had stopped crying now and was desperately looking around for some support from Queen Bob.

'Tonight has been a disaster, a tragedy, a joke!' continued Peter.

'*Nota for me,*' whispered Louie Marcello Bontenostrumienotto. The viewing figures were off the scale.

'I'm afraid you'll all have to face the fact that Evermore just can't make it in a modern world.' Peter was enjoying himself now 'It's out of date, it's finished, washed up.'

He rose to his feet. The crowd gasped. How he was enjoying this moment. He had them in the palm of his hand - he had everything, *he* had it *all*, he knew it would happen, he just hadn't thought it was going to be this easy.

'But all is not lost, my people.' He raised his hand with a flourish. 'I, Peter Piper and my **Piper Music** empire will save Evermore. For the final show *I* will supply the bands, the music and the talent.'

Throwing his arms wide he cried

'EVERMORE, I AM YOUR SAVIOUR!'

'I BEG TO DIFFER!'

A lone voice rang through the sound system, Queen Bob appeared in the beam of a single spotlight in the middle of the deserted stage. She was dressed in a simple grey hoodie and faded jeans.

'Eh...oh... what?' Peter had anticipated a storm of applause and a tidal wave of adoration. He had expected to be carried high on a golden throne through the streets to the Castle where he truly belonged. He hadn't expected this.

'*I've* got a band and my band are going through to the final.' She winked at Aspinol and gave him a look that said *who's a clever bird then.*

Momentarily Pete's stomach fluttered and his smile wilted slightly like a wet cardboard cut-out of Peter Piper. What band? There wasn't a band. This wasn't in the plan.

'There isn't a band,' he said, doing his best to conceal his bewilderment.

'There is now. A new band - a Girlband.' Announced the Queen. 'Come on out girls.'

From behind the curtain stepped four figures, Miss Muffet, Mary still holding her little lamb, Jill and Polly. Certainly not looking like the shy, nervous individuals who had performed it the first half of the show.

Miss Muffet was dressed in a one-piece bodysuit decorated with glistening spiders, Mary had a fleece mini dress and fleece boots (no lambs were harmed in the creation of this piece, although her little lamb toddling along behind her did look a bit bald in places). Jill strutted in wearing a sensational brown paper outfit and Polly looked amazing in Queen Bob's heart dress.

The crowd erupted, clapping and cheering and hollering and whooping and dancing and jumping up and down pretending to be elasticated wheelbarrows.

65

'Oh! ha-ha-ha-ha!' Pete chuckled, feeling relieved. Did she really think she was going to turn his world upside down with that style-less set of mismatched rejects? *HA HA HA HA HA!*

HA HA HA HA HA HA! Pete was almost doubled up now, slapping his leg in delight.

King Pants sat in the middle of it all wondering why he could smell caulicumbers.

HA HA HA HA HA HA!

Enough. Pete didn't want to overdo it - he'd made his point. He flicked a silk handkerchief out of his top pocket and patted his brow gently, hoping his expertly applied makeup hadn't run too much.

Up in the Director's suite Louie Marcello Bontenostrumienotto bounced around with joy.

'Theeze eez fantabella, superbo! What a spectaclurario. Alla we needa nowa isa punch in the Piperman smug faceo and we getta da Oscar maybe!'

'Is this allowed? Can we change the rules like this?' said Jack, although he wasn't sure who he was addressing, the director? the judges? It should have been the man in seat five row 'F' who had written the rules, but he was busy choking on a crisp.

'Don't worry, let her have her Girlband,' said Pete with curled lips. He had rethought his strategy. There was still an ace stashed away up his elaborately embroidered sleeve. 'But they will have to compete with **Piper Music's** most talented stars.' Trust Queen Bob and that skinny foreign bloke with the long neck to try and mess things up!

'I will show you the true meaning of the word talent!' said Pete, treating the audience to one of his most staggeringly fabulous grins and a closing wink.

' *EVERMORE, PREPARE TO ROCK!* '

The Queen could stand it no more and she said a rude word that had all the sound technicians in a frenzy trying to find the bleep button.

(too late!)

Still burning with rage, she began to lead the girls away.

'Before you leave, O' Queen of all our hearts, can you tell us what you intend to call this revolutionary "Girlband" of yours? called Pete.

'No, let me guess, it's more fun.' He placed a finger on his cheek, sarcastically. 'Hmm, something sweet? Something *sickly* sweet and sugary perhaps?'

Hilda the cook, sitting near the back, suddenly remembered she had left something in the oven and in all the excitement had forgotten to go and take them out 'THE JAM TARTS!' she screamed!

The audience roared their approval.

'The Jam Tarts!..

The Jam Tarts!' they chanted.

'The people of Evermore have spoken. **The Jam Tarts** it is!' Queen Bob gave Pete a withering look and lobbed the microphone in his direction hitting him in his gleaming, triple-plated, highly polished teeth.

Louie Marcello Bontenostrumienotto slapped his belly with delight and lit a huge cigar.

'Rolla on the creditos, that'sa the wrap!'

Chapter 18

The Night That Followed the Big Night Before the Following Morning

The house lights came on, the cameras were turned off, the stage was being swept and the orchestra were all sacked. The audience left in a disorderly fashion, shoving and pushing, desperate to swap their tokens for a delicious pie.

'Right, that's that, let's get to the after-show party,' said Pete, who despite the Queen trying to humiliate him was still grinning like a rat who'd just whipped the cream away from under the cat's nose. The microphone may have dented his pride a little, but nothing could knock the shine off his armour-plated pride and joys.

King Pants didn't even know there was going to be a party.

'I didn't know there was going to be a party!' he said as if to confirm that he didn't know there was going to be a party, which he didn't.

'Well, you should have" smirked the Piper "You're paying for it all!!!'

'I'll just go and find Bob,' sighed King Pants. 'I think she was a bit upset earlier.' (You have to hand it to him this King don't miss a thing.)

'Nonsense, that was just a bit of theatrical sparring, a bit of razzmatazz, showbiz bish-bash.' Pete said dismissively throwing air punches, 'I must admit she certainly knows how to work the camera.'

King Pants felt a sudden flush of pride. He had no idea that Queen Bob could operate such a hi-tech piece of optical equipment, but then again, she was always full of surprises.

'Come on, the party will be starting soon. She'll probably already be there.'

King Pants and Peter Piper were greeted like superstars when they arrived at the lavishly decorated ballroom. The King hoped this was the party he knew nothing about, because it looked *really* expensive, and he was quite sure he couldn't afford two of them. There were great platters of food piled high, rivers of various weird-coloured drinks. Fire-eaters, jugglers, acrobats, fancy cats in bowler hats, ballet dancers, clog dancers, ballet dancers in clogs, magicians, musicians, mathematicians with skin conditions and a donkey called Dave (Dave didn't really have a job so he just stood there looking confused). The recently fired orchestra had been newly re-hired and were messing up some favourite classics. All organised by Peter Piper and charged to the King's personal account.

Everyone was so excited. They waved, clapped and back slapped, they high-fived and down-lowed, fist-bumped, fist-pumped, air-kissed and did *The Twist* (knees bent, arms stretched) and bow-wow-wowed! A very large drink was shoved into the King's hand.

Louie Marcello Bontenostrumienotto gave a speech that nobody understood and then did a little Irish jig.

The King scanned the river of faces to see if he could see the Queen. While he was squinting a very large drink was shoved into his hand. He spotted Aspinol with **The Jam Tarts,** he saw Little Boy Blue, he saw all the other acts, except Tom Thumb. Over by the exuberant buffet he could see Jaqueline Sprat. Then again it would be hard not to see Jaqueline Sprat. But no Queen Rebobina.

Pete pulled King Pants into a quiet corner and shoved a very large drink into his hand.

'Well, KP this is even better than I could possibly have imagined, and I have imagined some pretty good outcomes all of which involved me, I mean us (he meant himself) getting absurdly rich and powerful. I … I mean we (he meant himself) I mean Evermore (he meant himself) is a *GLOBAL SENSATION!*''

The King was still looking for Bob, scoping the room like a remote-controlled egg whisk with a couple of gob stoppers glued on top. Jacqueline Sprat was just finishing off the last scraps of the buffet as a queue of disappointed partygoers waited behind her with empty plates and empty stomachs. He noticed the room had gone a little blurry and it seemed to be moving from side to side. But no Queen Rebobina.

'The final is now going to be incredible' continued Pete, excitedly shoving a very large drink into the King's hand. 'I've got the best bands, the greatest, rockingest and rollingest, hit makers *ever* and they are coming here, to Evermore, to take on Queen Bob's Jam Tart outfit. We're going to **SMASH HER TO PIECES!**'

King Pants wasn't very sure if he wanted to smash his Queen into pieces, but the room was now spinning clockwise and anti-clockwise at the same time and there seemed to be two of everything. He wondered why he was carrying two very large drinks in both sets of his four ten-fingered hands.

Pete was still talking, hardly breaking for a breath 'And now that you're a *Superstar* I want you to go on stage and introduce them.'

'**Meee**?' King Pants slurred, dribbling a bit.

'You'll be an overnight sensation. The TV audience will love you, the tabloids will love you, the world with love you!'

Despite being King of Evermore King Pants tried to avoid speaking in front of large crowds. And traditionally large Evermore crowds tried to avoid listening to the King.

But for some strange reason King Pants had a vision of himself standing bravely on a stage (wearing the most amazing psychedelic pants in the world) in front of a sea of adoring fans. The image throbbed in his brain like a thousand wombats fighting on a translucent trampoline.

'I dure ip'

[*Trans;* I'll do it!]' he said, taking another swig from his half-empty glass. '**B'ow whirly not f'slay?**'

[*Trans;* but how will I know what to say?]

The King's tongue seemed to be taking a nap and was hanging out of the corner of his mouth.

'Don't you worry about a thing. Just write down the list of bands I tell you and you'll be fine. You can fill in with some of your charismatic witticisms. Just be yourself,' Pete added with a snide smile.

He was now having to support the King who looked like he was about to collapse in a heap. He needed to be quick.

On signal, Tarquel (who was never far from Pete's side) handed the King a pen and paper and a very large drink.

'The first act is called **NOTHING LASTS**. Write that down first.'

King Pants sniggered.

'Bah's nunny nam borea bamt'

[*Trans:* That's a funny name for a band]
'They're alternative goth, grunge indie rock.'

King Pants sniggered again.

'Wimbdy spock'

[*Trans;* windy sock].

'Act two' pressed Pete 'are **FOREVER SUCKS**'

A sudden blast of projectile mirth gave Tarquel a centre parting. With distain he wiped the spray of spittle from his forehead and readjusted his fringe.

'Dey noent bound vo beeltu, *hic!*'

[*Trans;* They don't sound very cheerful, *hic!*]

The nib of the pen scrawled the words seemingly unguided by the King's hand as he slumped over the piece of paper Tarquel was now holding at arm's length.

'They're not supposed to be cheerful..' Pete said impatiently.

'Act three - **I'M A STAR NOW.**'

The King scribbled, trying to keep up.

Pete saw that the King was getting a bit *too* giddy. He'd have to be quick.

'Act four - **IT'S SO OVER.**'

'Ga, blon be bly blat Blete'

[*Trans;* Ah, don't be like that Pete]

King Pants began to croon, what he thought sounded like 'We've Only Just Begun...' in what he thought was a husky voice. It actually sounded more like a flushing toilet wrapped in whoopee cushions bouncing off the walls of a lift shaft.

'Just write it. Come on, quickly. And the final act - **BYE BYE CIAO BABY.** Write that down and then sign it. Now make a copy for the Queen.'

The wobbly monarch did as he was told, his handwriting was really wonky now and the punctuation marks floated around randomly, as did King Pants' eyeballs. But he did manage to add a nice little extra touch for his wife.

That'll cheer her up, he thought with a hiccup.
Pete Piper snatched the finish note to examine it.
'Perfect, just perfect.'
He read it out loud to himself, silently in his head.

Bob
Nothing lasts
Forever sucks
I'm a star now
It's so over
Bye Bye Ciao baby
King Edgar his majestic and most esteemed monarch of the
noble Kingdom of Evermore.
Your Ex X

Pete folded up the piece of paper and placed it inside his breast pocket.

'Don't worry, I'll keep that safe my little puppet and you'll be just dandy. Now, *LET'S PARTY!!*'

Pete shoved a very large drink in the King's hand and led him reeling into the ecstatic pulsating crowd.

Chapter 19

The Morning Following the Night that Followed the Big Night

One of the King's eyes peeled slowly open and the light of a new day streamed in with all the gentleness of a sharp stick. He could hear the blood pumping through his temples like angry bulls on space hoppers playing a game of basketball with bowling balls. He knew he was alive because his head hurt, and he could hear the Queen shouting somewhere in the distance. Although her voice was muffled, he could make out a few words and phrases.

'Hopeless!..... should have been supportive...made to look a fool...so...embarrassing....disgrace....Jam...Tarts....how....love....strangle....Pete....Piper....leaving....Goodbye..'

The eye had heard enough and slowly closed again.

Chapter 20

A New Chapter for the Queen

In the small hours of the morning when all the ranting and crying and ripping up and throwing things had finally ended, and while King Edgar still lay on his bed, snoring like a malfunctioning foghorn, the Queen said a final goodbye to Aspinol. There was tears and pleading, begging and heartbreak.

'Pull yourself together, you old softy' snapped Queen Bob.

She pulled an old and worn-out hat and cloak from the back of the wardrobe, sparked up a rollie and slipped out of the Castle. She had only made it a few yards before she was nearly knocked into a ditch by a reckless burger van.

'Oy, watch out!' she yelled shaking her fist. 'What's your problem, are you simple or something?'

Simple Simon waved back through the open window.

'Morning,' he smiled cheerily. Poor people are so friendly, he thought to himself, they have such little baggage.

And yes, crazy as it may seem, Queen Rebobina had now chosen to be poor, and she did indeed have very little baggage.

Everything she now owned had been hurriedly stuffed into a Tinker, Tailor, Soldier, Sailor Surplus Stores Bag for Life.

'Give it all away, sell it, or throw it in the moat, I don't care,' she had announced with a defiant sniffle before she left.

'But my Queen' protested Aspinol 'I feel reluctant to allocate such veritable fineries into such a classification that would warrant imminent disposal.'

They were standing in front of all the Queen's belongings, packed in bulging cases and overflowing boxes. Possessions and memories sealed away and silenced with a double wrap of sticky brown tape. Aspinol allowed his usual decorum to slip and wept openly. The Queen turned away to hide her own glistening eyes while she handed over the key to her shoe closet. (Queen Rebobina was very fond indeed of her extensive and expensive shoe collection.)

She looked down at the sunken mess that was the sleeping King Pants, recalling his words and wondering how long he been feeling this way.

Why was it all over and why now?

How could she have missed the signs?

Why couldn't he tell her to her face?

And the biggest question of all…

Did that sleazy slime-bucket pipe-blowing blood-sucking ratcatching ratbag have something to do with it ??????????????????? ??????????????

Plain Rebobina Scrump - that's who she once was then and was once again now. Not born into royalty or privilege she had always felt like something of a triangular prism-shaped peg in a hexagonal hole. Her family were cloth-makers and tailors from the land Far Far Away. They had only come to Evermore for the Coronation Day because it would be a bit of a knees up.

Prince Edgar had only spotted her because she'd gotten a bit squiffy and climbed up a lamppost and waved something that would be considered quite rude in polite society. That had been it and they had been together ever since.

The day Rebobina Scrump had become The Queen of Evermore had not gone down well everywhere or with everyone. Back then every Princess in the world was chomping at the bit to win the eligible Prince's hand. Princess Always from Never Neverland, Princess Cookie from Maryland, Princess Elvis from Graceland, Princess Buy One Get One Free from Iceland and Princess Penny from Poundland, each in turn had had a crack at becoming the next Queen of Evermore.

Perhaps that's where it all went wrong. Prince Edgar should never have been with a commoner. Was she now feeling the sting of his imperial entitlement. Was she no more important than one of his silly CDs, rejected just because he was bored and wanted a change? What would become of her now? Where would she go from here? Rebobina Scrump pondered these troublesome questions and many other enigmas of the Universe (like, is a muon a sub-atomic or elementary particle?) as she stuck out her thumb to wearily hitchhike her way out of her problems and away from Evermore.

Chapter 21

Back to the Morning Following the Night that Followed the Big Night

This time King Pants woke with a start.

Uuuurrrrrghhh! He tried to hold his head in his hands but missed and dropped it.

He had been having a funny dream about a party that involved a sheep.

As gradually as the whirring of his Grandfather's broken Grandfather clock in the Great Hall, his hazy mind started to become aware of his surroundings. Something was not quite right.

Why was he lying on top of the bed and not in it?

Why was he fully dressed and wearing a bonnet?

Why were all the wardrobe doors wide open?

Why were there torn bits of paper all over the floor?

Who had stuck a fork through his nose on the portrait above the fire?

And where was Bob?

These were all unanswered and mysterious questions, like in that whodunit novel the Queen had once thrown at him *The Mysterious Nature of Unanswered Questions* by Tom Foolery.

He climbed onto the floor and tried to stand up, but his legs crumpled beneath him. They felt almost as though he'd been dancing all night.

He looked around the room.

Where was his crown?

He looked in the mirror.

Why did he have lipstick on his cheeks?

He looked under the bed.

Who on earth left that there?

He looked at the torn pieces of paper scattered on the floor.

Who's been littering in my bedroom?

Then he noticed the pieces seemed to have writing on them. Ah, this could be a clue, he thought to himself (he would have thought to someone else but there was nobody there). Slowly he knelt down and began piecing the jigsaw together.

But why would Bob tear up the list of Pete's bands? It didn't make any sense. In a state of confused befuddlement he removed his lovely lipstick and pretty pink bonnet and headed outside.

He needed some air.

He needed some painkillers.

He needed some answers.

(Good luck with that!)

Chapter 22

Down the Shady Back Streets

A tall shady sinister-looking figure covered by a dark cloak with a hat pulled down over its face slipped silently out of the Castle grounds heading for the town. Tarquel came scurrying behind carrying Peter Piper's briefcase.

A few seconds later another mysterious figure with a big long neck and feathers, also wearing a cloak and hat pulled down over his eyes, slipped out behind them. It was Aspinol (in case you didn't guess) obeying the Queen's final instructions.

'Listen up Asp,' she had said as a salty tear dripped into her tobacco pouch.

Plip!

'Catch that slimy ratcatcher at whatever cost, he's up to something wicked I just know it! Now give me a peck on the cheek, I'm off.'

Aspinol had watched as she wrapped a dark cloak around her shoulders, pulled a hat down over her face and slipped silently out of the Castle.

And so, like a lanky, rubber-necked, long-legged clumsy ninja, Aspinol, now found himself hiding in shadows, jumping into doorways, ducking down behind and inadvertently toppling overflowing bins of stinking rubbish, muck, fag ends and fingernails.

Deeper and deeper into the shady back streets of Evermore he sank. He had never ventured this far from the Castle before, it was a strange world indeed. The smells, sights and the noises were far worse than any he'd ever encountered in the smelly marketplace.

'Oy Gets out froms them bins!' A toothless hag swinging a grubby half-dressed baby shouted.

'Yeh! Stops tryin nickin us food!' called a beast of a man with a nose and body of an angry bull.

Shadowy figure No 1, and Tarquel, turned left, right, right, straight on for a bit then right again and left into grotty sludge-stained alley. They finally stopped in front of a door that quite frankly could have done with a lick of paint. On the door, scratched into the rotting wood, were the words

Unit 13B Back Street Business Centre
Please go away and GET LOST!

Ignoring the polite notice, the shadowy figure slipped inside and Tarquel followed.

Aspinol crept noisily forward trying to be careful to avoid the broken glass, shards of metal and general debris that covered the alley.

scrunch

clang

squelch

Luckily, being an ostrich, he was one of the tallest birds in the world and stood approximately 2.49555 metres (or eight foot two and a quarter inches) high in bare feet. Therefore, he was easily able to put his head through a broken window above the door.

From this vantage point he saw the sinister cloaked figure remove his hood to reveal...*ta da*... Peter Piper! (Bet you never saw that coming!)

That comes as a merciful reinforcement as to the justification of my pursuit Aspinol thought to himself.

Phew!

Standing as still as an ostrich, he watched the proceedings unfold.

'I am looking for Simon.' Pete Piper announced to a man who was wiping a bogey on his grimy apron.

'Whos yous?' asked the man.

'Who are you?' Pete regarded the man with a look of distain.

'Thats was Oi sez.'

'I'll take it that you are the chef here?'

(The apron with the word Head Chef written on it was a bit of a giveaway.)

'Oi's the Pieman.'

'And that this is the FILLET LE CARRE PIE CO?'

'*Yers*'

'Then, my grimy, bogey covered little drudge, I am your boss, your employer. I am PETER PIPER!'

'Yous P-e-t-e-r-P-i-p-e-r?' The man became suddenly interested. Wiping his hands on his crusty, bogey covered apron he held it out in grovelling anticipation.

Pete backed away in alarm.

'Where's Simon?'

'Dunno Oi aint seens im sins yesturdy.'

Aspinol heard a sound like a cage door slamming. Quickly, he ran to another broken window and peered in. Once his bulging eyes had adjusted to the gloom, he couldn't believe the unbelievable horror that met his protuberant occular organs. Row upon row, cage after cage stacked high to the ceiling. Hundreds of fat, hairy, Filthy Lurkers munching away on great fistfuls of Ramblewortwood weed (the most addictive and fattening vegetation known to man). In the midst of all this a strange man with a nose like a dog carried cages in and out of door marked

PIE KITCHEN.

Aspinol began to swoon with nausea. This was all too much for his delicate disposition, he was after all a high-born bird of refined taste.

'I don't believe it!' he muttered in disbelief.

Back in the first window Peter Piper was shouting at the Pieman.

'I want a thousand more pies today and a thousand more than that tomorrow and if you can't do it, I'll find someone who can. Now give me the recipe.'

'Not der secrets recipe?'

'Yes, yes, the secret recipe. What else, you imbecile?'

'Buts that's der secret... TOPS SECRET 'tis.'

'I know it's top secret, hush-hush, restricted, classified, blah, blah, blah. But you signed it over to me, you fool. Don't you see it's MINE, I own it. Show him Tarqs!'

Tarquel held up a huge, leather bound, complicated-looking contract and pointed to clause 116c in sub-section 4, paragraph 97, sentence 43.

'*SEE!*'

The Pieman didn't see. He just shrugged his shoulders and sniffed.

'If you don't give it to me, you'll be in breach of contract. Have you any idea what that means?'

The Pieman had absolutely no idea what it meant but felt pretty sure it involved hanging upside down. He wished Simon was there so he wouldn't be able to explain the finer points of corporate contracts to him. Reluctantly he reached into his pocket, pulled out a screwed-up piece of paper and handed it to Pete who unpicked as timorously as if it was soiled toilet tissue.

Aspinol would later describe the noise that came out of Pete's ears, nose, mouth and eye sockets at that moment as a wail of demonic proportions.

IS THAT IT?!!!

he bellowed. Spittle-coated rage flew in all directions.

PASTRY!
GRAVY!
MEAT!

Aspinol ran all the way back to the Castle at top speed, 70
Kilometers per hour or 19.44 metres per second (or 43 and
a half miles per hour).
Wow! that's fast!
and stuck his head down the toilet.

Chapter 23

Some Fresh Air, Some Answers and More Questions

In Aaaaah! **and out,** Aaaaah!
In Aaaaah! **and out,** Aaaaah!
King Pants breathed in a couple of lungs worth of fresh clean air. Suddenly he felt much better. Everything seemed to be as it should. Birds were singing, bees buzzed lazily from flower to flower, the sun shone brightly and a girl wearing a crown was being sick against the walls of the Castle. What? Wait! What? Instantly the King felt a lot worse again.

'Miss Muffet? is that you?'

He was sure he recognised her from the talent competition. Little Miss Milly Muffet looked up into the King's blood-cracked pupils through her own blood-cracked pupils. She wiped her mouth with the back of her sleeve.

'Wotcha KP, howya doing?' she said forcing a wonky smile. 'Hey girls look who's here!'

'Hey KP,' hailed the rest of **The Jam Tarts** who were heaped together on a bench as if they had fallen out of a tree.

'KP? Excuse me, I'm KING EDGAR, reigning monarch of Evermore!' King Pants said indignantly. He attempted to stand up straightish and put on his noblest voice.

'That not what you said last night Old Mr Silly Pants,' laughed Polly.

'Last night?'

He was beginning to fear that his memory banks were not fully up to date.

'At the party, man,' chipped in Mary.

'KP, this is you right' Jill stood up precariously on the bench curled her lip, bent her elbows up and squatted her legs wide. She began to rotate her hips in exaggerated circles, thrusting and gyrating. Her legs and arms twitched in erratic spasms. Throwing her head back she shrieked into an imaginary microphone.

Hey, you cats, I'm a King, yes a King,
Just doin' my thing,
I wear a crown,
I'm a'gettin' down.
Just call me…
Kaaaaay Peeeeee!

She ended the performance with a rather spectacular high kick and a bow. The other girls squealed with delight at Jill's impressive impression.

Surely these hungover hellcats can't be the same four girls that Queen Bob had led off stage the night before.

'You're all insane! this is treason!' King Pants exploded with rage. His face looked as if someone had pumped red paint up his nose with a high-pressure drain plunger.

'I'll have you all thrown upside down in the dungeon!'

'Oh yeah! Well, what about Antoinette?' snapped Mary.

'Antoinette? Who on Earth is Antoinette?'

The King silently begged his brain not to remember.

'I don't know anybody called Antoinette,' But memories of the night after the big night before were now dripping into his consciousness like an awkward runny nose.

The night had started off quietly with a few drinks…

He'd had a chat with Pete about something…

Watched the dodgy fire eaters and incompetent jugglers…

Listened to speeches he couldn't understand and some unrecognisable music of questionable accomplishment…

But no Antoinette.

'Antoin*nnnnette*,' sang Mary with a little whistle.

From behind the bench stepped a rather sheepish looking figure (sheepish being the operative word since Antoinette was indeed a sheep). Mary's little lamb to be precise.

King Pants looked at the sheep.

Funny haircut, he thought.

The runny-nose memory trickle now turned into a full-on sneeze. His head whooshed with flashing, distorted and disjointed images from the previous night. Massive clinking glasses filled with lurid coloured liquids overflowing with laughing faces. Pete, Jaqueline, **The Jam Tarts,** Tarquel and a donkey called Dave.

He'd jumped on a chair and made a few speeches … sang a few songs... and hugged a few people.

Innocent enough.

No worries so far.

He remembered throwing his arms around Jack Sprat, that Irish chap and a few girls. OK lots of girls, all of them in fact, and a few hairy roadies. For some reason he remembered having an in-depth conversation about a nasty bum rash.

And then a little game of spin the bottle that involved River dancing in a pink bonnet (so that's why his legs ached so much), pretending to be a zombie vacuum cleaner snorkelling in a bath full of custard creams and cellotaping Tom Thumb to a lampshade.

Nothing too shameful.

At this point reality hit him like an iceberg. An unavoidable, slow-moving and seriously chilling monument. He remembered the bit where he threw his crown into the crowd shouting 'Who wants to be King?' before scuttling around on all fours pretending to be a giant spider with Milly Muffet riding on his back.

Oh no, no, no.

And finally kissing a lamb who was wearing red lipstick.

Ah! That would be Antoinette then!

'*Pants, pants, pants!*' he jabbered, shaking his head as though trying to shake off the memories his brain had just assaulted him with.

But it was too late.

Despairingly, King Pants sank to the ground.

How could it have all gone so wrong?

Why didn't I just leave things alone?

What happens now?

And the biggest question of all…

Did

Pete Piper have anything to do with all this???????????

'Snap out of it KP,' said Miss Muffet clicking her fingers in the King's face.

'You can have your stupid crown back. I never wanted the job in the first place. Come on girls. I knew all this was too good to last. Nothing's ever gonna change around here. It's just boring old King Pants in boring old Evermore. Same old fairy tale.'

Picking up his crown, he carefully wiped it clean and placed it on his head.

It was still a perfect fit.

But was *he* still a perfect fit for the crown?

King Pants experienced a rare moment of existential awareness.

King Edgar of Evermore was his title.
But **King Pants** was what they called him.
In their eyes he was a useless fool.
A joke of a King.
And now he'd proved them right.

The girls began to drift away. King Pants began to cry.

After a few quiet sobs time seemed to stand still. It didn't really stop - the leaves on the trees continued to grow, water flowed downhill towards the bottom, the earth still continued to spin headlong towards its ultimate destruction by crashing into the Sun.

But something shifted.

None of it seemed important anymore.

'Wait!' he called after the girls. 'I have to find the Queen.'

Polly turned back and waved her dolly at him. 'We're looking for her too. We need her. She brought us together and promised to turn us into something. She promised to make **The Jam Tarts** a world-class band. We'll help you look. Let's try the burger van.'

'Burger van?'

'It only arrived this morning. Everyone from the party's there getting some food. Someone must've seen her, there's a queue a mile long.'

They all headed off in the same direction.

'Hey! Your Majesty,' chirped Jill, 'You couldn't lend us a few shepples could you? We're starving!'

Chapter 24

Bobby

Rebobina Scrump had trudged her lonely way along the road that led from Evermore to everywhere else. The Castle and surrounding town were now just a blot on the horizon. She thought it strange that she would never set foot there again.

Already she was bored and homesick and tired and hungry. She kicked a perfectly innocent little stone along the side of the dusty road, wondering what was going to do with the rest of her life when...

Beep beep!

A huge shiny black mobile home with blacked-out windows pulled up beside her. The distraction was a great relief for the little stone who quickly skuttled back to his family.

'Where are you goin' doll?' a drawly voice called from the unusual vehicle as one of the darkened windows slowly lowered.

Rebobina looked curiously at a long-haired unshaven man. He was wearing what looked like a hairy multi-coloured tie-dyed t-shirt with a **Take it easy on the Hippies** slogan on the front. As she moved a little closer, she realised he wasn't wearing a tee shirt at all. It was his skin!

'Where am I going? she shrugged. 'Anywhere that's not here!'

'Well jump right on in, that's where we're goin' too,' said the man. 'Anywhere's only somewhere that ain't not nowhere!'

She looked up and smiled. Maybe she'd just found her tribe. Weirdos, outsiders, carefree folk.

What have I got to lose, she thought. The stranger opened the sliding side door. In she climbed, maybe her adventures were only just beginning.

'I'm Chad and this is Sally.'

Both Chad and Sally were equally long haired and sported slogans on their chest. Thankfully Sally *was* wearing a tie-dyed t-shirt. Emblazoned on the front were the words

I HATE HIPPIES

'Hey!' nodded Sally

'And this is Lennon,' (also weird.)

'Hey!'

'And Lake,' (*Whoah! Freaky!*).

'Hey!'

'And we are.... **BYE BYE CIAO BABY!**'

They all cried in unison pulling demented faces and sticky-up fingered hand gestures.

Rebobina nearly turned and fled, but something sparked in her mind... **BYE BYE CIAO BABY?**

'Yeah! The world's loudest, happy hippy, acid trippy, New Age rock band. You must have heard of us!'

'Of course, I have,' admitted Rebobina. She wasn't lying. She'd heard their name only that morning. Her gaze drifted towards the back of the van. Sitting there in the gloom were four totally silent, miserable-looking figures. They looked like an ancient black and white photograph of long abandoned and unloved porcelain dolls. A chill ran down the ex-Queen's spine. 'And who are they?' She pointed.

'That's **FOREVER SUCKS**' said Lennon 'They're not very cheerful.'

'What's your name doll?' asked Sally.

'Qu..er Rebo...' the Queen paused to think.

'Bobby!' she answered, with a small smile. 'Where are you actually going?'

'Evermore of course man.'

'We're gonna rip the place up. Peter Piper says he's gonna set fire to the backwards little kingdom and rebuild it in his image. Apparently that crazy King with the crazy hairdo (Chad pulled his hair out at crazy angles) thinks some ragtag, made-up girl band can take on **BYE BYE CAIO BABY** in a talent contest!' Chad snorted. 'And he says the pies there are far out!'

'Look, we know the Piper's a creep,' added Lennon, 'but he says we're all going to be working for a millionaire by next week.'

'Does he indeed?' asked Bobby thoughtfully.

'May I ask, have YOU ever been to Evermore?' said Lake, who was surprisingly polite for someone who looked like an insane floor mop.

Bobby rolled her eyes and settled back into a plush leather bean bag seat.

'Oh yes. I been to Evermore all right!'

Chapter 25

Over at the No Meat Whatsoever Burger Van

'Roll up, roll up get your lovely, tasty, vegetable, meat-free burgers, absolutely no meat whatsoever, one hundred percent pure meatless vegetation,' called Simple Simon from the hatch in the burger van that had only just narrowly missed knocking over the Queen that very morning. (Oh! that burger van).

The No Meat Whatsoever burger van was doing a roaring trade. Simon had thought up the idea the previous evening following his fruitful conversation with Mr Bulbhead. Once he had realised his dealings with King Pants and the Pied Piper would probably mean he was going to spend the rest of his days hanging upside down in a damp dungeon with no telly, he immediately spent his illicit earnings buying the mobile kitchen.

He decided that the *no meat* policy would be a good way of distancing himself from the FILLET LE CARRE PIE CO'S immoral wrongdoings.

'There you go Sir,' he said, handing over another succulent snack to another hungover reveller. 'Did I mention that there's no meat in there whatsoever, only lovely vegetables.'

'And one for you Miss? There's no meat in there, you know. Not a sausage.'

'Would you like a meat-free burger too, sir?'

'Of course you can eat vegetables, madam. I don't care what they taught you at school!'

Without warning Betty Botter, who was doing the cooking, dropped a huge pan full of meatless vegetables on the floor with a theatrical *Clang* and dramatic *Thud!*.

'Your Majesty!' her jaw fell open as she hurriedly curtsied, all a fluster.

For the face she faced at the hatch was none other than that of His Majesty the King, King Edgar himself. He had been standing impatiently in the queue half an hour to get to the front.

'Oh Your Royal Highnessness I'm ever so sorry I am you must think terrible of me what with you and the Queen being so nice and all and taking me in and giving me a job and all but I was going to tell you honest I was but I couldn't find you don't you see or the lovely Queen bless her and Simon here was getting ever so busy so he was and all and he asked me and that and I said yes so I did and he's been ever so nice so he has and he says that when he has got some money and that then we can get married so we can and then we can live happily ever after and all that just like you and the Queen bless her do and all that.'

Simon (not so simple that he didn't realise what was going on) gulped.

This was it.

The game was up.

He was surely going to spend the rest of his days hanging upside down someplace, or worse.

But the King just smiled wearily, hardly looking at Simon.

'Never mind Betty, don't worry. I just need to ask you, have you seen the Queen?'

'Your Majesty that is what I have been telling you and that I haven't seen her since the wee small hours so I haven't and even then I didn't see her but she was shouting ever so loud so she was so I heard her so I did and she was in a dreadful state so she was bless her and all that.'

'Would you like to sample a humble burger, your most Royal Magnificence?' grovelled Simple Simon relieved that he might have got away with it. 'There's absolutely no youknowwhat meat in them, I swear. Here, have this one on the house.'

'No thank you,' said the King. 'Perhaps you could feed these girls, they've had a long night.' He gestured at the group of unkempt **Jam Tarts** by his side.

'I hope you do find her so I do.' Betty called after the sad-looking monarch 'Try the maze I would. I know she likes to go in there so she does if she got things on her mind and all that.'

Chapter 26

Try The Maze I Would

With Betty's words still ringing in his ears and the smell of vegetable burger grease in his nostril hairs the King set off in the direction of the maze. He didn't dare stop on the way in case he got caught up in another unnecessary storyline.

It had been a long time since he had played inside the perplexing network of topiary hedges. As a boy he had never really learned the layout and had become even more confused when his nanny had suggested he should know it like the back of his hand. It looked nothing like the back of his hand, or anyone else's hand for that matter.

As he entered, he recalled a younger, happier King playfully chasing Queen Bob around the perennial puzzle for hours on end - whiling the days away without a care in the world, pretending not to be lost but never worrying about finding the way out, knowing she would always rescue him…eventually. Once, during a game of hide and seek it had taken five hours for her to find him, and when she finally pulled him out of a bush by his nose she was wearing a brand-new dress and her hair was a different colour.

Now he stumbled around the leafy labyrinth with a heavy heart, realising he didn't know the way out and his Queen was not there to rescue him.

'**Pants!**' he cried upon another fruitless turn.

'**Pants!**' Another dead end.

'Wait a minute, I'm sure I've been here before,' he said, standing at the entrance.

But which way do I go?

Should I go this way, can I go that?

Will I go forward, could I go back?

If I go up, can I get back down again?

Will I forever be lost without my Queen?

'Help I'm trapped in an allegory,' King Pants shouted at the sky, whose gaping span seemed to symbolise the limitless expanse of confounding possibilities.

'Where are you, Bob? Why do I keep getting flashes of existential self-reflection? What does that even mean? What colour is electricity? Has everything now changed forevermore in Evermore? What's the longest word you can make using a single tin of Alphabetti Spaghetti? Why so many questions?'

'Oh, come on scriptwriter, help me out here,' he said, falling to his knees.

'And a sheep, for goodness sake! What's all that about? Don't tell me it's another metaphor? Am I really so weak-willed and easily led?

Can I not make my own mind up about anything?'

He was at a loss. He didn't know.

He would have to ask Pete later.

A noise somewhere nearby dragged the King out of his mental maze of despair and desperation.

He followed it till he reached a clearing (a real one not a metaphorical one) where he found two plump-looking boys crouching on the ground and squabbling over a game of cards. The boys were identical in every way, other that one had a blackened left eye and the other had a blackened right eye.

'Excuse me, who are you, and what are you doing here?' interrupted King Pants.

The two oddballs jumped up, their legs wobbling as if they were noodles.

'He's Tweedledum' said Tweedledee, elbowing his twin in the ribs.

'And he's Tweedledee' said Tweedledum, elbowing his twin in the arm. 'And you're the...'

'...King,' said Tweedledee. 'Do you want a game of gin...'

'...rummy with us?' finished Tweedledum.

'I'm looking for the Queen have you seen her?' enquired King Pants, already suspecting that the answer wasn't going to be straight forward (he was having that kind of day).

'The Queen?' cried Tweedledee.

'Of course, we've seen the Queen.'

'Everybody's seen the Queen,' continued Tweedledum stamping on his brother's foot.

'I've seen her here,' said Tweedledee.

'I've seen her there,' said Tweedledum.

'We've seen her over there.' They both chirped in unison, pointing in different directions.

'I've seen her under here.' Tweedledee lifted Tweedledum's hat. The two were clearly a pair of nilly-ninks set on outdoing each other. They started to run around frantically pointing up and down and into flowerpots, on top of benches and behind bushes.

'JUST TELL ME HOW TO GET OUT OF HERE!' shouted the King, whose hopes of ever finding any sense or the outside world again were fading faster than his favourite denim pants in one of Hilda's hot washes.

The twins stopped in their tracks.
'That's easy,' said Tweedledee 'Just follow your...'
'...heart,' said Tweedledum. Then they shut up.
King Pants, who'd had quite enough enigmas, metaphors and allegories for one day, was none the wiser. Both boys lifted their stubby arms, and the Kings eyeballs followed the direction in which they pointed. Just above the hedge, twinkling in the sunlight he saw the clear outline of a golden heart. The Sweetheart Fountain! Of course...

He had commissioned the piece for Queen Bob when she had first moved to Evermore. It depicted the Queen holding aloft a heart. Around the bottom of the memorial a reaching figure of the King tried to retrieve it. He never really understood what it all was supposed to mean, but he suddenly felt overcome by the burden of fate.

Right in front of the statue was a massive **EXIT** sign with an arrow pointing the way out.
How had he missed that!

'Stay and play with us we're going to have...' said Tweedledum punching Tweedledee in his right eye.
'...a fight,' continued Tweedledee, punching Tweedledum in his left eye.
As their eye's slowly blackened, they became identical again and universal order was restored, if only for a few seconds.

'I'm going to kick your...' a full-blown scrap broke out.

'Well, I'm going to slap your….'

The King was already gone. Following the direction of the golden heart and the big **EXIT** sign. He was out of the maze quicker than a Filthy Lurker chasing his squeaky supper down a sewer-pipe and heading back to the Castle with a new determination to make amends.

As he passed the area of the Castle grounds where all the bands were noisily practising for the Grand Final of *EVERMORE'S GOT TALENT* (just in case you had forgotten about that) he had a fleeting thought to look in there for Queen Bob.

'Nah,' that's the last place she'd be, he concluded.

It was, of course, exactly where she was.

Chapter 27

Back at the Fillet Le Carre Pie Company

The ovens in the squalid little factory kitchen were steaming, sweating and chugging out great belchloads of thick black smoke. Day and night, they never stopped spitting out pie after pie just to keep up with demand as orders flooded in.

Equally as relentless as the pie orders was the relentless need for more Filthy Lurkers. Dognose even had to make up with his arch-rival Carrotnose to reach agreement over hunting rights far and wide in order to acquire more of the disgusting beasts.

The Pieman, after wiping another bogey on his grimy apron, had just stepped outside to scare off some hungry children when something caught his eye - the front page of **The Evermore Gazette**.

While the newspaper-seller was distracted (chasing off some current affairs enthusiasts) the Pieman sneakily nicked a copy and hurried back to the factory with his ill-gotten gain.

'Oy's Dognose!' he shouted above the shouting, chewing and farting of the Filthy Lurkers packed in cages stacked at the back of the dirty backroom.

'Cum'n ere an' sees dis.'

'Wat's it? Oi's bizzy!'

Dognose walked into the kitchen wiping Ramblewortwood weed off his blood-stained hands with a stinking blood-stained rag.

'Dis!' The Pieman held up his stolen copy of **The Evermore Gazette**.

Dognose squinted. There, splashed across the front page was a huge photo of a drunken King Pants landing a big gooey smacker on the puckered lips of a lipsticked lamb.

'BAAAAD KING IN SHEEP DIP!'

Dog Nose read the headline out loud. 'Ant we met 'im? 'E looks loike dat bloke wat comed 'ere'

'No, not dat!' snapped the Pieman.

On the same page was an advert for the FILLET LE CARRE PIE CO with a picture of Peter Piper giving a double thumbs up. 'Aah, dat's noice dats is.'

'No, not dat!' snapped the Pieman.

Dog-nose slowly read the next article.

'EVERMORE BALLOONS! Reports are coming in that the average weight of the average citizen of Evermore has jumped on average over 20% in the last week. 'We just don't understand it,' said dietary scientist Brainy Brian McKnowall. 'Even I have had to buy bigger underpants and I only eat three pies a day. It's a complete mystery!'

'No, not dat!' snapped the Pieman.

Only two days now until the Grand Final of *EVERMORE'S GOT TALENT,* sponsored by the FILLET LE CARRE PIE CO. Next to it a photo of Peter Piper giving a double thumbs up.

'No, not dat!' snapped the Pieman, stabbing a grubby finger at a small article near the foot of the page.

Dognose sighed and read on.

'Local entrepreneur, and all-round good eggy headed citizen Simon Simple is single-handedly taking on the scourge of the junk food industry by opening a vegetable only absolutely no meat whatsoever meat-free burger van in the grounds of Evermore Castle.'

Dognose stepped back in shock.

'You's carn'ts be serious! Who's gonna eats fings wif no meat!' he laughed.

'Don't yous gets it!' shouted the Pieman. 'Simon Simple is Simple Simon you's muzzle snozzled dimwit! 'Ees rund orf wi us money's.'

A few minutes elapsed before the shepple finally dropped. Dognoses snout twitched with fury.

'Oil kill 'im Oi wills!'

'Oil do's worsen dat,' joined in the Pieman. 'Oi's gona feed's 'im to da biggerist fattyist filfiest Filthy Lurker. Den Oi's gona cook's dat Filthy lurker in a durty ol'pie. Den Oi's gona eat's dat pie, Oi is. Den Oi's…'

Dognose thought it best to stop the Pieman at this point. (Otherwise, this book would be censored and placed on the naughty list).

'Les go ger 'im!'

'Ay, lets!'

Off they both marched with hate in their hearts, revenge on their minds and bogies and blood stains on their aprons and hands.

'Ee muss 'av gon apopsuittelly crackinpot int 'ead barmy mad.' said Dognose, shaking his head with disbelief.

'Imagerine finkin' yous can eats vegetablets!'

Chapter 28

Let's call the whole thing off

Eventually the King arrived back at the Castle where Aspinol accosted him in the great hall.

'Your Majesty, your Majesty!'

The gangly bird was flapped like an oversized rubber glove in a hurricane.

'I have established and collated substantial evidence that would incriminate a certain personage of your acquaintance in the illicit marketing and supply of contraband food products. And I have taken steps that may necessitate the involvement of the appropriate regulatory enforcement authorities.'

'Good for you Aspinol, you just carry on with that then,' said King Pants. 'I' and 'food' were the only words he could make any sense of within Aspinol's rambling oratory, so he naturally assumed it had something to do with lunch.

'You haven't seen the Queen, have you?'

The bird fell silent and shook his undersized head, unable to stem the single tear that fell from the tip of his beak onto the polished marble floor, *Plink!*

Oblivious, King Pants bounded on through the Castle checking in all the rooms. He would have checked all the Queen's favourite hiding places, but he didn't know where they were.

Meanwhile Pete had just finished having his teeth polished and was admiring his good looks in the mirror. Tarquel was taking off has safety shield and shutting down the industrial grinding machine when the chamber door dramatically swung open.

'KP! Where have you been, and where's the Queen?' asked Pete in a tone of sincere concern. 'We've been so worried, haven't we?'

He winked at Tarquel.

'I don't know,' started King Pants. 'I mean, I know where I've been obviously... kind of, but I don't know where Bob is, and I don't know if you have been worried.' He tried to remember if there were any other things he didn't know.

'All I do know is I've been out there, in all that madness, searching for Rebobina all day. Real people are.... INSANE!'

The King's eyes were shot with such utter desperation that Tarquel had to turn his gaze away. Even the manipulative Piper felt a fleeting sprinkling of compassion. But it was quickly supressed by his raw avarice and egotistical ambition. That was all that mattered. Mustn't cave now. The plan he had originally devised was now long, long gone in the broken dustbin of discarded history, but fate had smiled on his nefarious soul. This was a scenario far better than he'd ever expected. Nothing could go wrong now.

'She'll be back. It's not like it's the first time she's sulked off in a huff,' Pete said, breezily. 'Remember that time when...'

King Pants did remember but he wasn't going to be reminded just now, thank you very much.

'THAT'S IT! We have to call the whole thing off until I can find her, or until she comes back or next Wednesday.' The King paced manically round the room with leggy strides like those of a constipated ironing board.

'It's no good, I just can't do it without her. My mind's made up. I'm calling the whole thing off! It's over!'

Prising his eyes from his own reflection, Pete swung round to face the King.

'Whoooah! Wait just a ninnyplinking minute!' he interjected jumpily. 'No need for such haste KP.'

King Pants was not listening, he was already instructing an incredibly odd-looking servant to call a live press conference. He would imminently address the nation, imminently, or sooner if necessary.

Pete froze. This was serious.

'STAGE FRIGHT!' interrupted Pete. 'That's what you've got, a simple case of stage fright. No shame in that, it happens to the best of us.'

His greasy hand slithered around the King's shoulders like a python eyeing up a fat Eudar. 'The bands are already here, and the show has to go on, with or without you. Do you really want to let everybody down? What would the Queen think of you then?'

King Pants certainly didn't want Bob to have an even lower opinion of him than the one he thought she already had. But, for the first time he could remember, probably ever, he had made a decision all by himself. And it felt good.

'Step aside Pete,' ordered the newly empowered monarch. 'I have a nation to address.'

Peter Piper turned a shade whiter than albino Eudar milk. Maybe all was not lost. Maybe it could still all go terribly right.

'Tarqel, I think we may need that flute after all,' whispered Pete as King Pants was leaving the room.

Tarquel nodded knowingly.

Outside the sky darkened.

Chapter 29

What!!?!

The Sun had disappeared again, as happens most days in Evermore. The huge outdoor stage specially built for the final concert was brightly lit with dazzling lasers and brilliant spotlights. Luckily someone had brought some along and knew how to plug them in.

High on the ramparts sat Bobby among her new friends **BYE BYE CIAO BABY**. Chad Chainsaw was the charismatic lead singer, Sally Vation played a guitar like no one Bob had heard before, Lake of Fire smashed the drums like an absolute animal and Derek Lennon played the bass. The day had been an explosion of excitement, music and endless rehearsing. Bobby had met all the other bands: NOTHING LASTS, I'M A STAR NOW and IT'S SO OVER. They were all brilliant, cool and enthusiastic.

Once Bobby had explained her plans for the big night even **FOREVER SUCKS** couldn't wait to get involved because the one thing they all had in common was a loathing of their sneaky, money-grabbing creep of a boss, Peter Piper.

As they all sat there, sharing a bottle of dark brown beer and a funny-smelling roll-up, one of the King's servants (the really strange-looking one) came to the centre of the enormous stage. With great pomp he ceremonially rolled open a rather impressive-looking scroll and spoke into the mic.

'   !'

he announced and started to walk away.

One of the Roadies ran on and picked the servant up by what may or may not have been an arm, carried him back to the centre of the stage then went and turned the mic on.

'Ehem!' the servant started again. 'Ehem!' For someone who looked as though their head hadn't been quite correctly attached to the bits underneath, he had a surprisingly commanding voice.

'Ehem!'

'Yes, it's working now, we can hear you,' said the lady in row 419 who was knitting a balaclava for her pet gecko.

He slowly unrolled the scroll once more. 'Ehem! His Highness, the most Majestic and esteemed Monarch of the noble Kingdom of Evermore, King Edgar is due to make a worldwide, televised announcement regarding the *EVERMORE'S GOT TALENT* Grand Final in exactly one hour. Don't mention that it has been cancelled... Oops! Sorry didn't mean to say that bit!'

The servant turned a purply-maroon colour, rolled up the scroll and in a flush of embarrassment, rushed off stage.

Gasps of shock, horror, astonishment, disappointment and incredulity swept around the auditorium like one of those things where everyone takes it in turns to stand up and then sit down again and it looks really good. Then again it was not like that because this was DEFINITELY NOT GOOD.

Chad quickly turned to Bobby with an even more crazy than usual look in his eyes.

But Bobby was gone.

King Pants had changed into his full 'King' outfit (the one with the robes and the furry bits) plus his 'special' crown (not the regular everyday one). He was looking forward to settling down in his favourite chair with a mug of hot cocoa and a … what WAS that? He sniffed at the cowpat-shaped object on his plate and took a little nibble from the edge. He wondered if it was one of those pies that everyone was on about.

'Hell's teeth, THAT'S DISGUSTING!' he spat 'I hope that didn't come from the pie factory me and Pete invested in.'

He turned back to the mug of cocoa instead.

It had been a long day. More things had happened than he had the energy or memory cells to remember. Through the window he could see the spectacular light show playing in the sky above the stage in the Castle grounds. He sure was glad that he had decided to call the whole thing off.

He wiggled his toes and sank back into his favourite chair. In just under an hour's time, he told himself, he could finally relax.

'**BOO!**' Queen Bob jumped out from behind the curtains.

'*Whaaaah!*' screamed the King almost doing a somersault.

'Bob! You almost killed me!'

'What are you screaming about you big sissy? It's only a bit of cocoa,' giggled Rebobina.

King Pants hopped around the room holding the front of his steaming robes away from his skin. He looked like he was riding the wrong way down an escalator on the front of an angry rhinoceros.

'Where the **pants** did you get to?' the King asked angrily, sitting back down in a warm, wet, brown, chocolatey patch.

Squelch!

'What's it got to do with you?'

She splashed some ruby red vintage reserve wine into the bottom of his chocolate-stained mug and began stirring it with her finger.

'I had some thinking to do.'

'Thinking? You take all your clothes and shoes and leave without a word? I'd say that was pretty thought*less*!' he punctuated his sentence with a stern grimace and a pointy finger. He was rather pleased with that one!

Bobby grabbed the pointy finger and bent it all the way back.

'Owwwww! That hurts!' cried the King.

Queen Bob remembered something, and quickly made a mental note to find Aspinol before he gave away or sold all her shoes.

'I'm not the one who crawled in at four in the morning with lipstick all over their face, wearing a pink bonnet, and with funny little notes hanging out of their pockets. Am I?' accused the Queen.

'Oh Bob, it's a long story, but I can probably explain,' whimpered the King with a face as long and as guilty as a fork full of noodles.

'No need, I've already spoken to Mary, and the rest I worked out for myself.' Queen Bob smirked.

'Forget about all that. I'm here to tell you NOT to call it off. The Grand Final I mean.'

The King looked confused.

'I thought that's why you left,' he simpered.

'It was and it wasn't, but all that's changed. Just don't call it off or I will fry you in your own hair oil, hang you upside down in a dog bin and then get everyone and everything that can breathe to walk past and stick bits of mouldy cheese up your nose.'

(And believe me, she would as well).

'Now…gotta go. Must shoot, work to be done,' she spat the remains of the wine and chocolate blend back into the mug.

'Work?'

'I've got a lot to do before tomorrow night. I'm going to teach that two-faced, grinning backstabber Pete the phoney Piper a lesson., you just wait and see!'

And with a final squeeze of his cheeks and a killer dead arm punch, off she skipped, singing:

With a Baa, Baa here and a Baa, Baa there.
Here a baa, there a baa,
Everywhere a baa baa.
Old King Pants he had a lamb. Ee i ee i O!

King Pants smiled. Everything was back to normal. And he was going to have the bruise and a sore finger to prove it.

Chapter 30

Citizens of Evermore lend me your ears

Once again, it seemed that the tiny, insignificant and previously irrelevant Kingdom of Evermore was on everybody's minds. Once again, the world was expectantly tuning in to **EBC**, this time to hear The King's Speech. Once again, the gossip mill was spinning like a demented frisbee in a turbo-charged tumbledryer.

'I say old bean, I do believe that funny King Pants chappie is having second thoughts about the Grand Finale of that jolly decent talent competition in Evermore'
'Well, I say, that would be most disappointing!'

'Voulez mon Ami, ooh la la c'est le Reginald Pantaloons en duex pesanter joleaux grande finale au Evermore' 'Et la non bon amour dans moa moa!'

'Actung alt bohne, dat Kinky Pant ist doing thinky no no fur der gejollen talenter grossen Final aust Evermore' 'Dat ist sehr boo boo und nicht guten!'

'Eh gringo, molo Panty Kinko de no no aventi jololo mucho mucho Fianali Evermore' 'Donto muchachios cambra noncho plip plip!'

'Naka domba funto, do bango jango finonko Kinko Pantopant bim Evermore' 'Dambo nombi buko ninibendu wah wah!'

King Pants sat on the edge of his giant throne, legs swinging nervously in mid-air. He had changed his clothes once again and was now wearing what looked more like a bathrobe than his regal ermine-lined state occasion clobber.

The lights were all set. The cameras were all set. Jaqueline Spratt's stairlift was all set. Louie Marcello Bontenostrumienotto sat in his Director's chair shouting orders at the lighting and camera technicians.

'Wadaya mean ya alla goodi to go? You no da say wheni ya alla goodi to go! I say wheni ya alla goodi to go! OK, nowi ya alla goodi to go, see!'

A huge, illuminated clock on the wall ticked and tocked down to the live broadcast with an ominous certainty and a repetitious ticking sound.

Tick tock!.

In the shadows up on a balcony overlooking the scene below stood a shadowy Peter Piper and Tarquel.

'This is it, Tarqs,' Pete hissed to his loyal underling, his eyes aglow with the anticipation of glory.

'My finest hour and the final blow for King Pants.'

'But Sir,' enquired Tarquel 'I thought you wanted the Final to go ahead?'

'I did. I still do. It still will. Don't you get it? Any minute now he's going to make a total fool of himself in front of the world. Everyone wants to see the Final and this lovesick halfwit is just about to cancel it!'

Peter's grin was wide enough to span several time zones.

'They're going to hate him - despise him. He'll be cast out like an outcast. He's lost his Queen, now he loses his Kingdom! And now that I've redesigned the FILLET LE CARRE PIE CO packaging with my face on the front of it *and* cut KP out of the deal, I will be INVINCIBLE!'

'Tarqs, you just sit back, relax and watch me go, not only to take over Evermore but the global, world, Earth planet!'

Tarquel was expecting a maniacal cackle but instead Pete put his hands beneath his chin as if posing for a glossy front cover photo shoot.

Tarquel couldn't help but feel a little sorry for the poor fool of a King, but was much too sensible, loyal and scared to let it show.

'Anda Trio, anda duo anda unio!' called Louie Marcello Bontenostrumienotto.

'ANDA ACTIONONI!'

The little lights on top of the cameras all turned red. The TV screens of the world flickered to life revealing a very sombre and understated-looking King.

'People of the world…' he read from a quivering sheet of paper, '…Citizens of Evermore, lend me your ears.'

'You ain't getting my ears, you monster!' shrieked Jumbo from the elephant compound.

'Nelly! Nelly!' he called, 'He's after our ears now!'

Nelly who was already running around in a state of complete panic spiralled into overdrive and knocked over a double-decker bus full of penguins on a day trip.

King Pants continued (hopefully this time without any interruptions).

'I come here this evening to speak to you all about the Grand Final of *EVERMORE'S GOT TALENT*.'

'What? No way? Who would have guessed that? Certainly not me, or the police, or Detective Obvious from the CID's Special 'What's the King going to announce that everybody already knows about task force!' flounced Samuel Sarcasm, sarcastically.

Back to the studio.

'The past couple of days have been a strange time for our beloved Kingdom. We have seen great change sweep over our land. What we used to consider *The World Out There* is now within these walls.'

He swept his arms to the sides as if to indicate what walls were.'

'I have spent this evening reflecting on whether I (pause) we, are ready for change. And I came to the decision that we (pause) I, was not. I decided to call the whole thing off and return to a time before change when we were all sheltered, unthreatened, simple…'

'Who are you calling simple!' shouted Simon at the telly. Betty, who was sitting on the sofa next to him, giggled.

'Where we all enjoyed an untroubled independent existence. We were innocent, contented, and quite frankly…' King Pants rose to his feet and ostentatiously threw off his bath robe to reveal a pair of skin-tight leather jeans covered in sequins and a frilly silk shirt in mauve, opened to the waist, revealing a large gold pendant on his skinny little chest.

'Very, VERY BORED!!'

'But tonight, that will change.'

Throwing his arms out wide he tossed back his head and cried,

'Tonight, Evermore… PREPARE TO ROCK!'

The cameras cut away to beam live images from the super-sized stage outside, perfectly timed (well done Louie Marcello Bontenostrumienotto) to catch Sally Vation hit the opening chord on her guitar with all the explosive force of a million dynamite-stuffed rubber ducks. Lake of Fire hit the drums like they owed him last week's pocket money. Chad Chainsaw reached a raspy high note that would make a choir boy blush and Derek Lennon strummed the bass. Lights, lasers, fireworks and theatrical smoke-bombs filled the night sky. All the good folks and the bad folks spilled from their houses, cottages, hovels, caves, boltholes, slink holes and shoe boxes and headed to the Castle to catch the unfolding event with their very own eyes.

The air was electric. The cameras cut back to the studio, King Pants was ecstatic, his face appeared on the vast video screens that towered above the stage.

'Let's show the World,

EVERMORE ROCKS!'

he shouted, punching the air with his fist.

In the auditorium the crowd erupted.

KING PANTS ROCKS

EVERMORE ROCKS!

KING PANTS ROCKS!

EVERMORE ROCKS!

The entire population was going mad, apart from Mad Frank the mad monk who had decided to have a night off and was curled up on a rock with a bedtime drink. Boy, would he be mad when he found out what he'd missed.

Louie Marcello Bontenostrumienotto dabbed his raw eyes with a tear-drenched handkerchief.

'Bella Perfectionato! Cuta, cuta righta der!' he whimpered adoringly.

The camera lights dimmed and TV screens faded, but the party in Evermore lasted long into the night.

'DRAT, DRAT and DRAT!' stamped Pete Piper as he watched the amazing spectacle. 'How did he manage that?'

Chapter 31

The Day of the Grand Final

After a sleepless night, Peter Piper was furiously stomping around in a furiously bad mood all morning. Not like one of his usual petulant strops, this mood was deepest black, and had stuck to him all morning like a stick of old black sticky liquorice that had been nailed on with 'Déjà vu' (a brand of) magnetic superglue. Reading reviews of the previous night's concert wasn't helping.

Breaking news **THE KING IS COOL – *it's official*–**
The Evermore Gazette
Not So Sheepish Now! King's Pants Steals the Show! –
Headbangers Weekly
The Rex *that ROCKED!* – *Musik Poop*
PROBABLY THE MOST SPECTACULAR TROUSERS TO EVER GRACE THE MUSIC SCENE–Fancy Fashion - Special Pants Edition
KING PANTS ROCKS! – News of the Universe

The Price of Onions Set to Rise, SHOCKER! - The Daily Allotment.

He had ripped up so many newspapers and magazines that his fingers were beginning to ache. He had kicked Tarquel so many times his foot was beginning to ache.

'At least you still have your pie empire as reward for your efforts, Sir,' reminded Tarquel rubbing his bruised backside.

'And the final of the Talent Show to look forward to.'

This was true, Pete took some comfort from the fact that he was due to make a pastry-encrusted fortune from the FILLET LE CARRE PIE CO, and he still had the enjoyable prospect of watching Queen Bob and **The Jam Tarts** fall flat on their frivolous faces. But these things didn't compensate for the disappointment he felt by being outsmarted by that hapless nincompoop, King Pants. He could still hear the rapturous chanting ringing deep in his ears.

KING PANTS ROCKS!

EVERMORE ROCKS!...

He covered them with his hands and took another swipe at Tarquel, this time with his left foot.

And what about those traitorous troubadours **BYE BYE CIAO BABY?** He owned them – they were *his band* and now they seem to be playing along to someone else's tune.

'I'm going for a walk to clear my head and do a bit of scheming and plotting!' snarled Pete, before storming out of the room to see if he could find someone else who deserved a good kicking.

Tarquel let out a sigh of relief, glad to be left alone for a few moments. At least it would allow a bit of time for his bottom to heal before the next onslaught.

'COME ON THEN!' ordered Pete from outside the door. 'WHAT ARE YOU WAITING FOR?'

Outside a big clean-up operation was in full swing. The discarded leftover wrappings of the previous night's celebrations were being collected in huge bins. Servants with long poles were trying to dislodge items of discarded underwear from the top of the Sweetheart Fountain. Cans, bottles, packets and picnic paraphernalia bobbed buoyantly in the boating lake.

Following their arrest for fighting Tweedledee and Tweedledum had been given a Community Service sentence and were crawling around on their podgy knees polishing gravel.

'I've already done that bit!' said Tweedledee poking Tweedledum up his nose.

'So have I!' said Tweedledum smacking his brother in the bum.

Pete got busy straight away and was just tipping the contents of another rubbish bin onto a flower bed when something caught his eye.

Surely not! Could it be? Yes, it surely was. The head was the right shape and the ears stuck out at all the wrong angles. That sly Simple Simon! It *had* to be him.

Hidden in a trash-strewn rosebush the Pieman and Dognose were spying on the No Meat Whatsoever burger van, menacingly.

'Oi tolds yous it was 'im,' whispered the Pieman wiping a bogey on Dognose's back because he wasn't wearing an apron. 'Im wot's took arf us monies an' not dun no's work.'

'Lez go's get's im an put's im in a sack,' urged Dognose.

As they emerged from the shrubbery and began slowly slinking towards their prey, the Pieman noticed another familiar face who also seemed to have set their sights on snatching Simon Simple. Yes, you guessed it - none other than P-e-t-e-r-P-i-p-e-r himself. The odious bakers froze in their tracks.

'Let's us wait'n'sees wot's ees ups toos,' suggested the Pieman 'Oi rekons ees gonna do Simon in 'imselves.'

Peter Piper did indeed intend to 'do Simple Simon in.' He was getting sick and tired of being out-foxed and double-crossed. Ever since he'd arrived in Evermore things had never quite seemed to go the way he had malevolently intended. Well, this time he was going to make someone pay. Nobody, and especially not this nobody is wriggling out of a dirty deal made with Peter Piper. The very man that had gone missing from *his* pie factory with a half a mound of *his* (well actually, the King's) money.

Pete cracked his bony but well-conditioned knuckles.

'*Vengeance,*' he hissed '*is MINE.*'

He stalked the van like a praying mantis sneaking up on an unsuspecting hard-boiled egg. As he drew closer, he could taste the sweet acidic smell of revenge, or was it frying vegetable burgers?

'*Sweet, sweet revenge,*' he growled, silently pushing customers out of the way.

Closer still until he was able to read the badly handwritten signage.

thE nO mEAt whaTSoever BurgEr vAn

'No-meat burgers!' thought Pete, 'Now, there's a business opportunity!'

The Pieman and Dognose watched from a distance eagerly expecting someone else to do their dirty work for a change.

That would be nice!

The villainous Piper had circled his way round to the back of the burger van. *'Vengeance!'* Pete whispered this time, *'Is mine,'* his eyes narrowed to slits, his hand rose with outstretched fingers reaching for the door handle...

WHACK!

'OY YOU! Whatever is it that you do been trying like that all shifty and that creeping around back here and all,' yelped Betty Botter wielding a burger flipping fish slice like a flipping baseball bat and slapping Pete straight in his sinister sneer.

'I just saw you just pushing that little girl bless her cotton socks on the floor down there so you did you should be ashamed of yourself so you should and now look she's all crying and that bless her little curly hair so there and you are a big bully so you are and all that and don't let me catch you sniffing around here again any time soon or again or I will give you another taste of my flipping burger flipping fish slice so I will.'

To Dognose and the Pieman this was the funniest thing they had ever seen in their miserable lives, and they both collapsed in a fit of uncontained schoolyard giggles.

Just watching Betty Botter expertly slice and dice P-e-t-e-r-P-i-p-e-r made them immensely happy and immediately forget all thoughts of carrying out any evil misdoings themselves. They were both still laughing like a pair of hyperventilating horses when they were hit by a heavy litter-laden garbage truck.

'You can come out of there now my dear so you can and all,' called Betty climbing back into the burger van. 'I won't let that horrid old stinker of a mean mugger come anyway near you so I won't you just see that fake smiley slimer won't get round your Betty so he won't I will see his shiny teeth coming from a mile off so I will.'

Simon climbed out of the fridge, shivered and gave Betty a big hug.

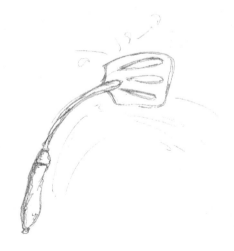

Chapter 32

The Night of the Grand Final

Peter Piper returned to his room in the Castle in an even more furious, if that were possible, mood than the really furious mood he had been in before he had gone outside to relieve his furious mood. It didn't help that he had a bright red mark on his cheek that was the exact shape of Betty Botter's fish slice.

'Start packing Tarquel!' he barked 'We're getting out of here the second this is over! I should've known better than to set a single foot back in this pathetic land of archaic aristocracy, maniacal monarchy, decrepit dynasty, stupid..er sovereignty, this…..(he was struggling now)…er…rubbish ruler reign..thing! And Tarquel.'

'Yes Sir?'

'You better have packed my flute, if you know what's good for you,' threatened Pete.

'I did, Sir.' admitted a weary Tarquel.

'I've got a funny feeling I might need it the way things are going. Now come and help me get ready!' Pete snapped.

'And don't forget the *Flawless Finish* concealer stick… the big one!'

'*AND NOW!*' a great voice boomed.

'*LIVE,*' it boomed again.

'Iffa we gotta do a this show againa, no more wid da boom boom it take a too long!' complained Louie Marcello Bontenostrumienotto.

'*THIS IS THE BIG ONE!*'

BOOM

'*WELCOME TO...*'

      BOOM   *BOOM*

'*EVERMORE'S..*'

           BOOM

'*GOT*'

    BOOM

'*TALENT*'

'THE GRAAAAAND...'

      BOOM

'*FINAL!*'

    BOOM

Just as King Pants and Peter Piper were being welcomed to their judging seats (there was going to be very little judging, Pete had already decided the outcome) up pops Queen Bob looking happy and relaxed, smiling and waving to the audience. She was still wearing the same pair of old jeans and hoodie (these were the only clothes she had left).

Pete Piper scowled crossly. Not another unexpected turn (as if!) He was still in a beastly mood but tried to smile as if it was all perfectly natural. King Pants was obviously over the moon.

Jack Sprat was his usual buoyant self, jumping and skipping like an escaping lunatic tap-dancing in a cat litter tray full of drawing pins.

'WELCOME, WELCOME!'

Jaqueline wasn't with him tonight as she had been rushed into last minute surgery to remove a bucket of deep fried Lesser Dotted Foulpig tripe that had gone down the wrong way.

'I must say you're looking very pretty tonight, Pete,' winked Jack at the Piper.

As the cameras went in for a super-close close-up Pete blushed a blotchy purple colour and the outline of a burger flipper on his still-smarting left cheek could be seen shining through his heavily applied concealer.

The audience hooted with hysterical laughter.

'Well then, let's get the show kicked off, shall we?' announced Jack.

'First up, please give it up for one of the planet's darkest Goth bands. Be prepared…be prepared to be…well a little bit depressed I suppose. Are you ready for **FOREVER SUCKS**?'

As Jack walked off the stage all the lights went out, and then came back on. But only a little bit. In the ghoulish half-light stood four white-faced figures, perfectly still. A synthesiser began playing a single – long - droning note. And then carried on,

and on,

and on,

and then stopped.

And then the lights came back on, and the stage was empty.

Jack walked back on stage to an atmosphere of dumbstruck bewildered silence.

'Have they finished?'

'That was a perfect example of gothic noir minimalism,' Peter began to explain. Even he wasn't really feeling it.

'It's an acquired taste. Move on.'

'Next up, its over to you Queen Rebobina.'

Jack Sprat bowed like a wilting Rhubarb stem.

At last, something to laugh about thought Pete. He couldn't wait to see the pitiful look on the Queen's face as she was humiliated on national TV in front of millions. He flashed a glance in her direction. But she was just smiling back, looking oddly cool and quietly confident.

'Evermore!' The Queen rose to her feet.

'Some people,' she shot a look in Pete's direction, 'Said that our little Kingdom could never, *would* never produce a band that could rival those that exist in the world outside. Well, tonight, those doubters will be proved wrong - and a bit silly. Evermore, get on your dancing feet, make way for......

..................**THE JAM TARTS!**'

POPOPOWWEEEEE!!

The music slammed instantly into top gear and the lights did a berserk forward, backward, upside-down, spinney thing. Everyone sucked in air sharply as **The Jam Tarts** invaded the stage. Milly and Polly slammed out killer riffs on shimmering, blingy, diamanté-encrusted guitars as Jill pounded thunderously on a monster drum kit that rose magnificently out of the stage floor on a cloud of dry ice. Mary grabbed the mic and snarled savagely

'ROCK OUT SISTERS!'

The Jam Tarts were amazing, their timing was as impeccable as their make-up and their choreography as tight as their costumes. They were sassy and funky and exceptionally loud, and everybody loved them. (Apart from Pete, who hated them). The whole of the Castle was bouncing, everybody within its walls and many, many more outside and around the world bounced too. Smoke billowed, thunder-flashes flashed, flames licked, crowds cheered. The orchestra joined in with soaring strings and melodious horns, surprisingly both in time and in tune (for a change).

Evermore was indeed **ROCKING!**

Just when you thought things couldn't get any more exciting, they got even more exciting.

The rhythmic pulse of rotor-blades filled the air, and the shape of a huge helicopter filled the sky. It was (if you hadn't guessed) a huge helicopter! At the same instant a door at the side of the stage burst open and in rushed the Pieman with an official-looking man from W.H.I.F.F (World Health Inspectors for the Federation of Food), waving a FILLET LE CARRE PIE CO box. They were closely followed by Aspinol.

'Dat's 'im!' shouted the Pieman poking a bogey-tipped digit towards the judges' table and then wiping that same digit on an unsuspecting doorman.

'There's the dubious villain!' The big bird cried pointing at Pete and racing forward with an unusually assertive outstretched wing.

Pete froze in his seat with the uncomfortable look on his face of someone who had left it too late to go to the toilet. Tarquel leapt to his master's defence and sank his teeth into the ostrich's leg.

All around dancing turned to fighting, but the way the good folks of Evermore danced it was always hard to tell which was which and the W.H.I.F.F agents were blocked at the door. Fortunately, reinforcements were at hand and long ropes fell from the doors of the chopper hovering overhead.

Agents from S.Q.A.T (Special eQuipment and Tactics) abseiled from the helicopter, one of them landed on the face of a tuba player only to be hit over the head with a double bass.

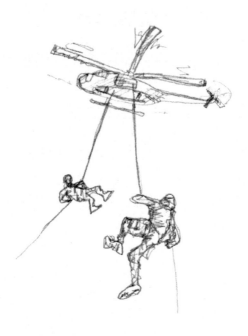

The music on stage pulsed with energy. Even the noise of the helicopter engine and spinning rotors above the crowd synchronised with and enhanced the funky beat. From all directions serious looking men in dark masks pushed through the fracas, fighting and dancing dubiously towards the Piper.

'*GET HIM, GET HIM!*' shrieked Aspinol.

And 'Has somebody got a sticking plaster and an Aspirin?'

Surreptitiously, Pete slipped under the table like warm jelly down a plughole. His creepy fingers crept into his inside pocket and wrapped themselves around his fiendish flute. The insidious instrument was, once again going to come to his rescue. Nobody and nothing had the willpower strong enough to resist its mesmerising melodies.

Emerging from his hidey hole, Pete licked and then pursed his immaculate lips, placed the flute into position and selected the keys he needed to achieve a hypnotic resonance.

'You'll never take me!' he mocked.

He took a in a deep gulp of air and then blew a slow, steady nefarious breath over the lip plate.

Nothing…not a peep!

He just had enough time to look down and notice that his blowhole had been stuffed full of Bobo nuts (small but highly affective due to their strategic placement) and then to glance over into the smirking eyes of Aspinol before a large S.Q.A.T officer called Steve, landed on him with the full force of karmic law.

'*Ooof!*'

The Jam Tarts rocked on regardless.

Chad Chainsaw joined Mary on the mic for a duet of *I love Rock 'N' Roll, Put another shepple in the Jukebox baby…'*

He ripped off his shirt to reveal his astounding tattooed artwork. Unfortunately, the lady violinist with the mouse phobia was equally scared of nipples and went screeching towards the exit again only to slip on a discarded FILLET LE CARRE PIE CO box and go flying over Tarquel who was now wrestling with an official from W.H.I.F.F called Mike. She eventually crashed into camera two knocking a cameraman called John out cold.

The remaining members of **BYE BYE CIAO BABY** joined in with *The Jam Tarts* taking the sound to new heights. All the other band members from **NOTHING LASTS, I'M A STAR NOW** and **IT'S SO OVER** (sorry, you didn't get the gig guys!) danced and clapped and cheered from the wings. **FOREVER SUCKS** stood at the back in the shadows.

King Pants and Queen Bob danced like a couple of carefree kippers on a windswept washing line.

'Brillianto, fabuloso!' applauded Louie Marcello Bontenostrumienotto as a violin smashed through the window of the director's suite.

Jack Sprat had been bopping around like a rubber octopus on a pogo stick ready to spring on stage and announce a winner. Since it seemed that this was now impossible and that no one no longer cared, he finally gave up and went to the hospital to see Jaqueline instead. You'll be pleased to know she had made a full recovery and was just tucking in to her third helping of the hospital's pudding of the day - Spotty Dick.

Chapter 33

Another Day in Evermore

The next morning the King and Queen of Evermore sat quietly at the long table in the Great Hall noisily scoffing a lavish well-deserved breakfast of applecurrent and bananaberry muesili with stacks of royal jelly-soaked pancakes, toast, all washed down with tea and glasses of weird green stuff.

They had seen the previous night through to the end.

'It's a good job those police people turned up when they did,' said the King picking up a piece of toast. 'Things could have got out of hand.'

'My girls were fantastic,' whooped the Queen, wiping the back of the butter knife under her armpit. 'They certainly wiped that smug smile off that prat Piper's face.'

Aspinol, wearing a bandage and limping slightly, entered the room carrying the morning papers.

'Listen to this, your Majesties. It says here, *Peter Piper is involved in, and was probably the brains behind, an illegal organisation trafficking Filthy Lurker meat. He managed to make a miraculous escape and has gone into hiding, but a spokesman called Mike from W.H.I.F.F (World Health Inspectors for the Federation of Food) said they will spare no resource, leave no stone unturned or pie box unopened in ensuring his early capture.'*

'Give it here, Asp, let's have a gander.' Queen Bob scanned the small print of the **Evermore Gazette** and poked the page with a jammy finger. 'You missed this bit, Asp. *It is all thanks to the King's special secret agent Aspinol that the operation was discovered, and the villains exposed.'*

The humble bird blushed proudly and did a neat little curtsey despite the painful teeth marks on his leg.

'Nice one Aspinol!' King Pants shook the bird firmly by the wing.

Queen Bob gave him a feathery high five.

'It was my pleasure to have been afforded the capacity to fulfil a necessary service to the realm and for the benefit of the greater good.' Aspinol then bowed again, graciously before dipping his head into a bowl of nuts.

'I'm glad it's all over and things are back to normal. I bet someone will write a book about all this one day,' mused the King.

'What sort of fool would do that!'

Seconds later King Pants dropped his toast on the floor. Fortunately, it landed butter side up, but unfortunately (for the King) it was swiftly stolen and devoured by a pair of lucky mouslets.

His face flashed white then blood-red then white again, and his jaw swung open like a slack-hinged cat flap. Transfixed, his bulging eyes stared over the Queen's shoulder. Queen Bob's stomach did a little flip as she turned quickly to look behind in order to discover the cause of his seizure.

Surely not the return of the treacherous Piper!

But no, there, at the door to the Great Hall holding a silver platter heaped with pastries stood Hilda the Housekeeper. Her vast folds of skin squeezed into a tiny dress. The entire creation was made from red silk hearts scarcely held together with large safety pins. (It's amazing what you can pick up in charity shops these days.)

The dress loomed towards them like an overwhelming haute couture avalanche.

'Anyone fancy a nibble?'

She placed the tray of pastries on the coffee table.

'Hilda, my favourite!' exclaimed the King.

'JAM TARTS!!'

And they all lived happily ever after (until the next episode) in Evermore.

The End

Thank goodness for that!

Epilogue

(What? There's more?)

In case you were wondering just what happened to that fiendish trickster Peter Piper (and I know I have been), well, there are reports that he was last seen, grinning like a loon, dancing a conga through the doors of The Pink Flamingo Nightclub in London's fashionable and notorious Soho district. He was accompanied by his slavish sidekick Tarquel, the Pieman and all the officers from W.H.I.F.F. He was, of course playing a tune on his diabolical flute.

The Jam Tarts, following their success on *EVERMORE'S GOT TALENT,* went on to be one of the largest grossing bands of all time. Hit after glorious hit propelled them to the very highest orbit in the star-studded stratosphere. Even Antoinette got her own reality dating show, *Kissing with Confidence.*

Simple Simon and Betty Botter made a fortune converting the good folks of Evermore to a vegetarian diet. They live in a modest two-up-two-down overturned laundry basket with their eleven children and a pet Eudar called Roy.

Dognose and Carrotnose have remained the best of enemies and can sometimes be seen throwing insults and small twigs at each other, as they skip merrily through the tall grassy reeds that infest the boggy wetlands of Evermore.

Although Aspinol remains a faithful companion to Queen Bob, he has recently become engaged to an emu called Cressida, who he met on a day trip to the Zoo. They are very happy together and the couple are expecting their first egg any day now.

Queen Bob and Chad Chainsaw are now owners and co-founders of the world's biggest, best and most nonexploitive band management, promotion and record production company, **'EVERMORE ROCKS'**.

She still teases King Edgar mercilessly; he still loves it, and she still loves him.

The rest is as they say, is all nonsense.

Oh! And Derek Lennon hopes, one day to have science's most extensive collection of microscopic ant dandruff flakes. He thinks he has at least 14, but he can't be sure because can't see them. He dreams of opening a museum one day.

About The Author

Noel J Brennan is a real person, honest!
He has spent most of his life messing around making stuff for Exhibitions, TV and Films. He has created scenery, props and sets for Raven, Gory Games, Reeves and Mortimer, Strange Hill High and the remake of the children's classic The Clangers. More recently he has been involved in SFX on The Dark Crystal and The Enola Holmes films.

In his spare time, he likes sculpting, painting, writing silly stories, playing the bass guitar badly and walking his poodle, Roy. He lives with his family in Cornwall.